NECESSARY ALPHA

Fire and Snow
Book 4.5

KHLOE WREN

Books by Khloe Wren

Fire and Snow:
Guardian's Heart
Noble Guardian
Guardian's Shadow
Fierce Guardian
Necessary Guardian

Dragon Warriors:
Enchanting Eilagh
Binding Becky
Claiming Carina
Seducing Skye
Believing Binda

Charon MC:
Inking Eagle
Fighting Mac
Chasing Taz
Claiming Tiny
Chasing Scout
Tripping Nitro
Scout's Legacy

Single Titles:
Fireworks
Tigers Are Forever
Bad Alpha Anthology
Scarred Perfection
Scandals: Zeck
Mirror Image Seduction
Deception
Mine To Bear

ISBN: 978-0-6483085-7-7

Copyright © Khloe Wren 2017

Cover Credits:
Digital Artist: Khloe Wren
Model: Deposit Photos

Editing Credits:
Content Editor: Carolyn Depew

Biography

Khloe Wren grew up in the Adelaide Hills before her parents moved the family to country South Australia when she was a teen. It was there that Khloe followed her father's footsteps and joined the volunteer firefighting service at 18. A few years later, Khloe moved to Melbourne which unfortunately meant she had to give up firefighting but she's always missed it. After a few years living in the big city, she missed the fresh air and space of country living so returned to rural South Australia. Khloe currently lives in the Murraylands with her incredibly patient husband, two strong willed young daughters, an energetic dog and two curious cats.

Khloe has always loved big cats, especially Snow Leopards. So it seemed only natural that when she began writing her first novel after having major surgery that left her on bedrest for six months, that she chose these beautiful creatures as her first shifters.

Chapter One

Rubbing a hand over his head, Finn didn't care he was making a mess of his hair. He did growl a little when some of the blond mess landed over his left eye. He really needed a haircut. His mother would start clicking her tongue at him if she could see him. But Finn didn't have the energy to care. He'd gone past tired and had entered the zone of being utterly exhausted, but still managed to muster the energy to drag his butt off the plane with all the other commuters who had shared the seven hour flight from New York to London with him. On auto-pilot, he somehow managed to make his way through Heathrow Airport. The entire trek through all the customs garbage and down to the baggage claim area, he barely noticed his surroundings. His level of fatigue became evident when he failed to notice the man dressed in full traditional Tibetan monk garb step into his path.

"Finley Taylor?"

Hearing his full name had him zoning back into reality. Shoving his hair back off his face with his palm, he eyed the man before him, trying to think where he recognized him from. He'd spent his last year traveling around Europe, and then America, trying to find his mate. Like all Snow Leopard shifters, Finn had started dreaming of her when she'd turned twenty-one.

That had been five years ago.

When he'd turned thirty last year, he'd been unable to resist the urge to seek out the beautiful golden-blonde haired woman he dreamed of every night any longer. His parents told him fate would make sure their paths crossed, but fate was taking too damn long to do its thing, so he'd headed off in search of her. The other thing his parents had drummed into him since he'd been a young boy, was that he needed to stay away from the Devon area of southern England.

Instinct had Finn wanting to defy them, to start his search there. After all, there was a leap in the area, so there would be plenty of shifters around. But proving how well his parents knew him, they'd made sure to tell him all about what the Alpha of the Devon Leap had been doing. Why they were living under the radar in the north of the country. They feared if the Alpha, Alastair, discovered their family had lived without his knowledge for so long, he would send his guards to kill them all. Well, they probably wouldn't kill his younger sister. That bastard Alastair would take her for himself. His father had told him about all the female shifters that had gone missing from the leap over the years, and the rumors of how Alastair had taken them to be his own personal sex slaves. Even worse, was his father couldn't give him the name of one single female that had ever been freed from his custody. What did the bastard do with them all? Or was it all rumor to cover up runaways? He shook his head. His parents wouldn't have left the leap over mere rumors. They certainly wouldn't have told him to avoid the area at all costs if they hadn't seen something along the way to prove Alastair really was that level of a bastard.

When Finn had quizzed his father on why no one had tried to take out Alastair, he was told all about the handy ability leap alpha's had. One that meant they could lock down any shifter they wanted, making it impossible for them to move their own limbs.

Anger had Finn's stomach rolling. An alpha shifter himself, his father had told him many times that he was sure Finn's destiny would be to be the Alpha of a leap of his own one day, somewhere in the world. But with the way his alpha instincts demanded he protect those around him, he could never imagine doing what Alastair had done, and was most likely still doing. How could any male, shifter or human, think it okay to steal away whatever woman who caught his eye, to keep under lock and key as his own personal sex slave? It was a level of evil he couldn't even imagine.

The monk before him cleared his throat, pulling Finn out of his thoughts.

"Sorry, I'm fairly wiped from all the traveling I've been doing lately. How do I know you?"

He smiled slightly with a nod of his head. "We are yet to meet in person. I am Choden. Did your father tell you about me?"

"Bloody hell!" Finn blushed at swearing. "Sorry, I didn't mean to curse. I know of you, but why are you here, looking for me?"

He realized he needed to choose his words carefully. They were in a public place, and with Choden in his orange robes, he was attracting some attention as it was. Finn shook his head in amazement. He could hardly believe he was standing before the original shifter. Choden was nearly three hundred years old, and had been involved with the original spell that created their breed. He couldn't wait to ask Choden exactly how that had happened, but now certainly wasn't the time, or place.

"I am, indeed, here for you. To discuss a matter of great importance." He looked around them briefly before returning his gaze to Finn. "Collect your baggage, then we will find somewhere private where we can speak freely."

Finn glanced up at the carousel to see his bag on its way around toward him.

"There's my bag now. Stay here and I'll be back in a minute."

He wasted no time grabbing his large rucksack and slinging it over his shoulder before returning to Choden.

"I'm sure we can find a quiet table in the back of one of the restaurants if you want?"

"I believe we need to speak for longer than that. Where were you planning on staying tonight?"

Finn rubbed the back of his neck. "Honestly, I'm so tired I was going to just crash at one of the hotels near the airport."

Choden gave him a nod. "Lead the way. We will speak once you have a room sorted."

Curiosity had him agreeing and leading the older man outside the airport and toward the first hotel he saw. Whatever it was Choden wanted to discuss had to be bloody important, because Finn's father had never even met Choden in person. In fact, on more than one occasion he'd expressed how he believed the man to be nothing more than a legend.

Finn couldn't wait to tell his father the legend was, indeed, real.

With her fists clenched by her sides, Brooke's body shook with rage.

"Someone has to stop that bastard! He's out of control."

"Sweetheart, what do you think Rick was trying to do?"

Tears stung her eyes as a shudder of grief rolled through her. She ran her gaze around the room, past her aunt, who was sobbing against her mate's chest as he held her. Then to her mother who clung to her little brother as though he, too, was going to try to take on Alastair by himself. And finally, back to her father, who stood before her, attempting to calm her down.

"Alastair is not fit to be called Alpha, Dad. Surely there's someone we can call in to deal with him."

"Every time someone tries to call in someone higher up, they disappear. Please, don't do anything rash. I don't want to lose you too."

Taking a deep breath, she forced herself to calm down enough so that she could hug her father. She had a bit of a reputation for being headstrong. Like the time in sixth grade when she got even with a trio of mean girls in her class by sneaking an old tuna sandwich into the bottom of each of their bags. Man, had it stunk up the entire hallway.

It had been totally justified in her mind. They'd been teasing another girl in their class relentlessly about stinking like fish because she always had tuna sandwiches for lunch. Poor kid was from a struggling farming family, it wasn't her fault that tuna was all her parents could afford. The fact all three of the bullies had to carry school bags that stunk of fish for the rest of the term guaranteed they got a taste of their own medicine. And they all learned that fish oil doesn't easily wash out of school bags.

Unfortunately for Brooke, her parents figured out she was the culprit, and they hadn't agreed with her methods of seeking vigilante justice. It was also unfortunate that something as simple as some smelly tuna sandwiches wouldn't solve the issues they all had with what Alastair was doing.

"Someone has to do something. This can't continue."

With her face pressed against her father's warm chest, with his muscular arms holding her tightly against him, she let herself go. Her tears soaked his shirt in seconds.

Shelley, Brooke's sweet, beautiful cousin, was still being held captive by Alastair, and her mate was now dead. Shelley had been snatched from her home to be their Alpha's latest mistress three months ago. For three months she'd been forced to warm that bastard's bed. When her twenty-first birthday passed last week, Rick stepped forward to her family to say he was Shelley's mate and was going to rescue her from Alastair's lair.

Brooke's uncle had warned him to not go in alone, but he hadn't listened. And really, none of them had expected him to. After all, what kind of male would sit idly by while his mate was being held against her will?

His mission had been a failure. Shelley's parents had received a phone call early this evening to say that Rick was killed for betraying his Alpha, and that if anyone else attempted to liberate Shelley, they would find the same, grim fate. Alistair would not be releasing her until he was ready. Which really meant until he found some other female who caught his eye more than Shelley.

With a shake of her head, Brooke pushed away from her father and turned toward the door.

"I need to go for a run."

"Don't you dare go anywhere near that house. Do you hear me?"

"I hear you, Dad. I'm not going to do anything stupid."

He didn't look like he believed her, but Brooke couldn't stay to placate him. She needed to vent her anger and she could only think of one thing that would calm her at this point. She jogged out of town, into the wilderness where she stopped and stripped down. Once naked, she bundled her clothes up into a tight roll. Then, standing back, she allowed the shift to overtake her. Blue light surrounded her for a few moments before she closed her eyes for a moment. When she reopened them, joy shot through her system at being in her snow leopard form once more.

She gave her feline body a good shake, and stretched before she lowered her head, and opening her mouth she carefully picked up her bundle of clothes. Then she was off, running through the trees and rocks, loving how the wind blew her silky fur back against her skin and the variety of scents that teased her nose as she moved.

She reached the cliff that was her destination and laid down to face the ocean. Dropping her clothes, she rested her head on her front paws and stared out at the crashing waves, pondering the situation.

Brooke's strong sense of justice and willingness to stand up for what's right translated into worry for her parents. They'd realized early on that she was destined to be the mate of an alpha shifter. They had both been terrified Alastair would scheme and plot to attain her. But it wasn't the case. In fact, Alastair seemed almost fearful of Brooke. He avoided her when he could, and certainly had never made any move to lay claim on her in a sexual manner. *I'd chop his damn dick off if he ever tried.* She winced. She knew that wouldn't be possible. An Alpha of a leap had extra powers over and above normal shifters—things like the ability to lock down other shifters so they couldn't move.

That was the real reason no one had ever been able to save any of Alastair's mistresses. He'd lock down anyone that came close to them, or him. How could she get around that?

Deep down, she knew it was up to her to end his reign of terror over her leap. It would have been nice if her mate had shown up at some point to help her, but after five years, she was sick of waiting and was going to do this on her own. It was a modern world, wasn't it? The Prime Minister and the Queen were both female and had been running things for how long now? Surely a female Alpha could run a leap just fine on her own.

The only thing she needed to do to make that happen was to take down Alastair and his goons. She laid on the cliff until the sun had set and the stars came out, her mind running a million miles trying to devise a plan.

There had to be one.

And she had to think of it soon.

Chapter Two

Tossing his bag into a corner, Finn pulled out a chair for Choden before he took the one on the other side of the small table in his hotel room.

"You know my father believes you're nothing but a legend. I'm going to enjoy telling him he's wrong."

Choden winced. "I apologize for never having met you or your family before. I found Alastair most unwelcoming to me, so I have avoided visiting." He paused to shake his head. "I had no idea what he was doing. I believe we will find he has been dabbling in magic of some kind. It is the only way I would have not known of his evil deeds."

Finn leaned forward to rest his elbows on the table. "What is he doing? I've only heard from my parents that he was taking mistresses as he pleased so they left to keep my sister protected. They asked me to start my search for my mate elsewhere, but I've been just about all over the world. I've seen no sign of her in a year of searching. I intended to go to the Devon Leap next, to look for her. Are you here to tell me she's been taken by Alastair as a mistress?"

Choden folded his hands and lowered his eyes to stare at his fingers a moment. "I could not tell you who he currently holds. I am different from all other shifters. As the original shifter, I am the only truly immortal one of us. I also see things that are to happen, or have happened. I wake in the morning and simply know. It is not always easy to have this knowledge, and there are many times I wish I could change it. But no matter how unpleasant, I always know what is happening with my leaps. Alastair has managed to stay below my radar. I knew when his mate passed, and I came to conduct her funeral. That is the last strong vision I've had of the Devon Leap."

"He lost his mate?"

With a look of surprise, Choden stared into Finn's eyes. "You know even less than I, it seems. I have come from the leap in Tasmania, Australia. They are going through a terrible time with the loss of their Alpha. Their new Alpha, Dominic is a good man. You would do well to contact him when this is all over. I believe you will both be good friends in the future, as you lead your leaps."

Finn lifted his palms. "Whoa! I know my dad always told me I was an alpha male, but I've never even lived in a leap. My family lives in the north and we keep to ourselves. We do everything we can to not draw attention from any leap. My sister is extremely beautiful, and has a gentle heart. Any man would want her and if Alastair is truly taking females as he wishes, he would snatch her in a heartbeat if he knew she existed. I intended to slip in and search for my mate quietly. If she's not there, I'll leave as quietly as I came. If she is there, I intend to take her with me. I was going to tell Alastair I'm part of a leap in Ireland."

Finn was certain he could pull off an Irish accent for a few days to play the part.

"I am sorry, but that is not your destiny. You are to be the new Alpha of the Devon Leap. It will be you, along with your mate, who will pull this leap back together."

Finn shook his head. "I don't know the first thing about running a leap. Let alone one that has splintered as this one has."

Choden reached across to place his palm over Finn's forearm. "I will always be here to help you, as will the other Alphas around the world. I may be old and not up with all the latest technology, but I do have a mobile phone that you can call me on. I will also introduce you to other Alphas, like Dominic. You will discover many will want to support you in your new role."

He still didn't understand. "Why would this Dominic want to help me? He's probably never even been to England."

"Dominic's good friend and leap brother is now mated to a woman who came from England, Rachel Bell. Her parents delved into magic to save their daughter from Alastair's attentions, then they supported her decision to go to Australia, as it put more distance between her and Alastair. Apparently, he began to show an interest in Rachel at a young age. It was Rachel who informed me of Alastair's crimes mere days ago. I came to deal with him as soon as I was able."

"How do you know I'm destined to be Alpha if you can't see what the future holds for the Devon Leap?"

Choden gave him that slow, gentle smile again. "On my way here, I sensed you, and who you were to become. I would guess due to all the time you've spent away from England recently, whatever magic Alastair is using has worn off you."

Finn didn't understand how the man could have put any magic on him in the first place. As Finn had, gratefully, never met Alastair.

"I'm not even going to ask. I've never understood magic, and don't want to start learning now." Especially when he had more important things to focus on. Like the fact he was extremely close to finding his mate. "Do you have a plan for how to get to Alastair? I'm sure others have tried to take him down before now, but he's still going strong by the sounds of things."

A wave of sadness passed over Choden's expression. "I, too, am certain others have tried, and it pains me that so many have suffered because of this one shifter. We need to go to him, at his home, and deal with him. I am sure I can dispel whatever magic he is using, and I can also counteract anything he does as an Alpha."

"You mean if he freezes me, you can free me?"

"Ah, you've been told of that trait. Yes, all Alphas that have been sworn in to rule over a leap have the ability to lock down shifters. It is designed for the Alpha to use to keep his people safe, but it is also only meant to be used in the most dire of circumstances. However, I believe you are right in guessing he is abusing this power. He will, no doubt, attempt to lock you down, and if he does, it will not work, as I will take the power from him as soon as I am close enough to do so."

With a wince, Finn looked at the clock on the wall. It was getting late, nearing eleven at night.

"You don't want to go right now do you? It's like a three or four hour drive to Lynton, and I'd really appreciate being able to sleep before we go."

Choden nodded. "Of course. I will go and begin to visit the shifters that have scattered from the leap. Maybe even those who have remained in Lynton. I need to start collecting information on what has been happening. I will return here as soon as I am able tomorrow afternoon. You need to be fully rested for our endeavors."

With that, Choden rose and left the hotel room. Finn sat in his chair, stunned for some time, before he could move to lie down so he could get some rest. Despite being beyond tired, he struggled to find sleep. His mind spun with information and possibilities of what he would encounter tomorrow.

Because he knew, no matter what happened, tomorrow was going to be a day of monumental change for him.

After her run the previous night, Brooke traveled to Alastair's house and kept it under surveillance for a few hours. It wasn't the first time she'd done it, and just like last time, she noticed that at around nine in the evening, the guards all vanished inside even though no extra lights came on. Had they all gone out the back and left for their own homes? Surely Alastair wasn't so confident in his security to have no guards at night? Even using her sensitive shifter eyesight, she'd been unable to pick up any movement other than in one bedroom. She'd avoided looking there, as she didn't need to see her cousin being used. Bad enough it was happening, no way did Brooke need images to go with it.

Now, in the light of day she was back to planning. Maybe if she snuck in late at night, after Alastair was asleep, she might be able to steal Shelley out of there without him knowing until it was too late. Maybe she should take a knife with her and slit the bastard's throat while he slept. She shook her head. She wouldn't risk that. If he woke, he'd lock her down and then who knew what awful things he'd do with both her and Shelley. No, later tonight she would slip in, free her cousin, and they'd both slip back out.

Brooke wondered if Shelley knew Rick was her mate and that he'd been killed trying to rescue her this past week. Would Alastair tell her? Had Rick made it close enough to have had contact with Shelley before he was caught?

Not for the first time she also wondered where her own mate was. Was he even British? Maybe she would be like Rachel, and need to leave the country to find him. She scoffed. Like it was actually an option. Rachel's parents had left the leap to keep their daughter safe, even going as far as using magic to hide her shifter abilities so Alastair would believe she was human, not a shifter. It did happen. It was rare, but every now and then, when a shifter mated with a human, their children would be human, not shifter.

It was only now that Rachel had found her mate in Australia, that her parents had sent word to Brooke's parents of what they'd done so long ago. They'd hoped Brooke's parents would be able to pass the information on to other families with young girls. To save more females from being kidnapped and forced into sexual slavery, and who knew what else, to serve their evil and twisted Alpha.

"Such extreme prevention measures, when surely it would be easier to just kill the bastard and be done with it."

"You're not plotting again, are you?" Her mother's voice sounded tired, and Brooke didn't want to cause her any more stress. But she couldn't lie to her either.

"Until the day that man is dead and buried, I will be."

"You can't solve this alone, sweetheart. He'll lock you down, then take you too. How will that help?"

Brooke walked over to her mother and wrapped her in a hug. "I'm not going to just storm into the place and demand he show me his throat, Mum. I'm trying to work out a way to sneak Shelley out without him even knowing I was ever there. Then, I don't know, maybe we can light the damn house up with him still in it."

Her mother gasped and thrust her away from her body so she could glare into Brooke's eyes. "Don't you dare! You won't get past his guards, and if you do and light that fire? He'd escape before he died, you know he would. Then he'd come after you. I'm as devastated about Shelley as you are, but losing you as well is not going to bring her back to us. It'll just cause us all more pain. Please, think this through before you do anything reckless."

"I have. I will. I told you, I have no desire to become his plaything. If I do decide to do anything, I'll be very careful, and I'll turn tail and run if I discover I can't get to her."

With a shake of her mother's head, Brooke was pulled back in for a tight hug. "You are going to be the death of us, Brooke. This need you have to save the world is going to make your father and me gray with worry."

"I'm not out to save the world, Mum. Just my family, my leap. And you're both already gray."

"See? It's happened already. If I can't convince you to not go, at least promise me you'll do all you can to stay safe."

She kissed her mother's cheek. Both her parents knew her well enough to know she would always do what her conscience told her needed to be done when it came to keeping those she cared for safe.

"Always, Mum. I always do everything I can to stay safe."

Chapter Three

Dressed head to toe in black, with her long golden-blonde waves pulled back into a tight braid, Brooke felt like she was on her way to audition for the role of a cat-burglar in a movie or something.

She wished she were.

Her stomach was in knots and her palms were slick with sweat, but she would not back out of her mission. Shelley had been living in hell for long enough. She glanced at her watch, the luminous display reading ten o'clock. That had given Alastair an hour after his guards left to do whatever vile things he did to Shelley each night. She had heard rumors that he never slept in the same room as his mistress. It made sense to Brooke. One of the females would have slit his throat by now if he let his guard down that much around them.

Blowing out a deep breath, she began to make her way up to the house, using shrubbery as shields when she could. Reaching the building with no problem, it was then time to try out her newest skill. About a month ago she'd started to research all she could about how to pick locks and then practiced every day until she was confident in her skills.

It really was amazing what one could learn on the internet.

She wiped her palms down her thighs before she slipped the two hair pins, that she'd modified earlier, out of the top pocket of her cargo pants. Licking her dry lips, she kneeled and focused her gaze on the keyhole of the lock. Remembering what she'd seen on the internet, and her hours of practice, she put the pin that she'd bent to have a looped end in the bottom of the keyhole and twisted to put pressure on the lock to turn it, then she slid the other pin, which she'd stripped the plastic off one end and slightly bent up the tip into the lock and began testing the barrels.

Sweat beaded on her brow as she carefully tested each barrel, pushing up the seized ones just like the man in the video had explained. The night was quiet enough that the click seemed overly loud. With a wince, she quickly glanced over her shoulder to see if anyone had heard it. When she confirmed she was still alone, her shoulders slumped in relief and she took a deep breath before she set about repeating the process with the other barrels until the looped pin twisted enough so that the lock popped open. *That really was way too easy.* She made a mental note to go shopping tomorrow to buy deadbolts to fit to all the exterior doors at home.

With the door now unlocked, she slipped the pins back in her pocket, in case she needed them later, and carefully opened the door before she slipped inside. After making sure it closed quietly behind her, Brooke slipped to the side to give herself a moment to get her bearings. From what she'd seen through the windows on her nights staking out the place, she made her way upstairs to what she believed to be Shelley's room.

She had one foot on the bottom step when she heard a muffled groan, then masculine cheering from below. The house had a basement? She frowned and debated whether to go check it out. From the cheering, it sounded like more than one man was down there. Was that where the guards were? She closed her eyes. *Please don't let that be where Shelly is.*

Taking a few deep breaths, she decided if Shelley was below, there was nothing she could do to free her tonight. She took another step up toward the bedrooms. She'd have a quick look in the room she believed was her cousin's, then she'd hightail it out of there.

Maybe she could sneak off one night and go to the Alpha of a neighboring leap to get help. Even if she had to go to France to find the Alpha of the Continental Leap, she'd do it. Whatever it took.

She made it to the door she believed was Shelley's and gently tried to turn the knob. It didn't budge, which made sense. Of course he would lock her in. Brooke pulled her trusty modified pins out once more and, kneeling, went to work on picking the lock.

But she made a mistake this time.

She became too focused on her task, forgetting to remain aware of her surroundings. So much so she didn't hear a sound before a hand wrapped in her hair and jerked her up from the floor.

"What do we have here? Another little mouse coming to the rescue so soon after the last? Did you think I don't have alarms set to warn me of intruders?"

His voice was deep and full of gravel, but it wasn't sexy in the least. Her stomach twisted and bile rose up her throat until she swallowed it down. What had he said? Something about an alarm? She hadn't seen any bloody alarms anywhere in the house. So yeah, she'd assumed he didn't have them. Forcing down the urge to gag, Brooke put a brave face on.

"I'm just here for my cousin. You have no right to keep her locked up here."

He chuckled. "Ah, so it's little Brooke that has come to visit me."

She frowned wondering how he hadn't seen it was her to begin with. Did he not have sensitive eye sight like she did? Before she could think that through, he had her back against the wall and his hand around her throat. As his fingers tightened on her neck, she tried to fight him off, but her limbs refused to listen. Panic had her heart racing in her chest and her breaths became nothing more than shallow pants as she struggled to get enough air in her lungs. She raised her gaze to his face and shuddered on the inside. She did her best to not focus on his eyes. She'd seen his irises a few times before, and every time she had, the sight of those nearly black, dead looking eyes had made her toes curl. And not in a good way. She focused on the top of his head, where the short tight curls were more grey than black, showing his age. Brooke wasn't silly enough to assume his age indicated weakness. He was anything but. At least not physically. His shoulders were broad and his biceps bulged with muscles. She frowned at that. She'd never been this close to him before to notice precisely how big his muscles were. His arms, in particular, looked too big. Was he on steroids or some other drug? Is that what had made him turn so evil? She'd overheard her parents and other older shifters say he never used to be like this when his mate was alive.

Using the hand around her throat, Alastair gave her a little shake.

"Nothing to say for yourself?"

"You... won't... get... away... with... this." Her words were a choppy croak as she took a shallow breath between each word. But he heard her just fine.

"Ah, that's where you're wrong. I've been getting away with it for a long time now. I'm the Alpha of this leap. I own every single one of you. That gives me the right to take anyone I please. Now, what to do with you..."

Cheers from below cut him off and he grinned, an evil expression that left Brooke trembling on the inside. "I could take you downstairs to join dear Becca. She's been the main attraction for my guards for three months now. I'm sure she'd appreciate a break. I know her mate certainly would. He's been watching her be used all night long for months. At least, when he's not being used himself. I imagine by this point they're both close to insanity."

Brooke's mind couldn't keep up. Becca was the mistress before Shelley. "Why would you do that to them? Why wouldn't you let them go free after the years she served you?"

He tapped her cheek twice, hard enough it was almost a slap. "That's simple, my dear. For punishment. Just like Rick, Becca's mate came for her, and she jumped from her window to him and they ran off. Of course, they didn't get far. I've got this whole place locked down with spells. Anyone can enter, but I have to allow you to leave. Once Becca and Toby reached the fence, they found themselves locked down. I had my guards go retrieve them, then I installed them both down in the basement. Now, every evening at nightfall, I put them both on lock down for the night and my guards are free to go have all the fun they want with sweet Becca and Toby. While I keep Shelley up here for my enjoyment."

Brooke frowned, trying to ignore her own predicament for the moment. Her thoughts traveled to Rick.

"Is Rick really dead?"

Alastair gifted her with another evil grin as he tore at her shirt, revealing her boring but practical sports bra. Hopefully he found it such a turn off, he'd leave her alone. She doubted he would, but a girl could hope.

"Oh, no. He's down there watching. Knowing that the day I replace Shelley, she'll be sent down there to join Becca. I haven't let my guards touch him yet, but at some point they'll tire of Toby and I'll let them at him. Quite the punishment, don't you think? If only you'd all left her alone, she'd have been free as a bird when I replaced her. Now, she'll never be free. Hmm. Let's see what we have here."

Brooke couldn't think of one single female Alastair had ever 'set free'. But before she could question him about it, or further think it through, he returned to tearing the rest of her tight black long sleeved shirt off. Once that was done, his fingers stroked over her breasts, causing more bile to churn in her stomach.

When he gripped the material between her breasts in preparation to tear it open, she screamed. And when she barely made a sound, she silently cursed his ability to lock her down. Not only could she not move, her vocal cords seemed to be affected too. She could talk okay, but yelling or screaming came out muffled. Or maybe that was some kind of spell he'd used, rather than part of the lock down. *Who cares?* Tears pricked her eyes when she heard the sound of material ripping. He was doing it slowly, clearly enjoying how she was reacting. She hated that he could tell how much he affected her, but she couldn't hold back the tears now. Not when she was about to be violated by this bastard while she couldn't even attempt to fight him off.

This was not at all how she'd envisioned her night going. How stupid had she been, all she'd done was compound Shelley's fate to one that was even worse. Alpha female, her ass. It didn't make any difference. He still just took what he wanted. Tears continued to leak down her face but she vowed the second she was able, she'd take this bastard out. All she'd need was one moment of his inattention and she'd strike out. So, she would stay strong and get through this, then after she somehow found a way to deal with the bastard, she'd find a way to escape from his guards – and she'd make sure the others were all with her when she did.

The Ford Focus Finn had rented to drive himself and Choden out to Lynton had done its job well, getting them to their destination in record time. Finn could feel deep in his soul that they were running out of time, so he pushed the tight-handling car to its limits. With Choden confirming his mate was in Lynton, he wasted no time following the GPS instructions to Alastair's house.

"Where do you want me to park? Around the corner so we can come in unnoticed?"

Choden shook his head. "I can deal with anything he tries to throw at us. Park in his driveway, near his house. I want him to know I have come to pass judgement on him for his actions."

When Finn pulled into the driveway, fear washed over him, stronger than anything he'd ever felt before. It had his heart rate racing and his palms sweating.

"Choden? I don't know what's happening to me."

The older monk frowned at him. "Your mate is in peril. You will feel her strong emotions, and you have no doubt felt them before, just not this strongly. Quickly, let us get around the back and into the house. I fear we are almost out of time to save her."

Not waiting for any more explanation, Finn threw open the door and sprinted towards the rear of the house. He quickly tried the handle, fully expecting to have to kick the thing in, but it opened easily. Frowning, but not pausing to think that through, he left the door open and continued into the dark house.

"Hmmm, let's see, what we have here."

He glided through the house, staying light on his feet, toward the deep, gravelly voice, that was vile enough it had the hairs on his arms standing on end. Staying to the edge of the staircase, to avoid anything that might creak, he was at the top in seconds. That was where all his good intentions to stay calm and handle things in a mature way that would reflect what an Alpha should do, went straight to hell. His beautiful golden-haired mate, who was even more beautiful in real life than she had been in his dreams, was up against a wall, clearly locked down as an older man slowly tore her sports bra down the center, revealing creamy swells that were destined to be Finn's alone. Her shirt lay in black shreds on the floor around her.

Finn growled in protest, the sound holding enough power that the floor trembled slightly beneath his feet, despite the fact that the actual sound didn't travel far. It was the furious call of an Alpha Snow Leopard.

"Get your fucking paws off my mate right now, you bastard."

The man, who he assumed was Alastair, spun toward him, a shocked look on his face. But he didn't look scared. He damn well should be. Finn intended to tear him apart. Finn tried to take a step toward Alastair and snarled when he found himself rooted to the spot.

"Oh look, another mouse has gotten into my house. When did you find your mate, Brooke? Are you keeping secrets from your Alpha?" With an astonishingly fast motion, he tore at her cargo pants. A growl vibrated up his throat at the sight. Alastair had removed a section of material that left her pants barely hanging from her belt. His mate's smooth pale skin around her right hip bone was revealed, along with the top of her pubic hair. "No mark yet. Are you playing hard to get, love? You really shouldn't, you know. You just never know how long you have left in this world."

The bastard ran a caressing finger over her hip and Finn saw red. He screamed out for Choden to unlock him, but because he was locked down, his voice didn't carry as it would normally. He attempted to frown. Choden hadn't mentioned anything about his vocal cords being affected by being locked down. Was this part of the magic Choden had guessed Alastair was using? Either way, he didn't need to worry, because a moment later, he felt Choden's presence behind him. A palm on his back freed him of his lockdown.

As he broke free and lunged toward Alastair, several things happened all at once. From below there were sounds of men screaming and animals growling, while in front of him, his mate fell from the wall and leaned down to snatch a knife from her boot.

Alastair's fatal mistake was ignoring Finn's glorious mate. Like an avenging angel, she silently rose up behind the evil Alpha and with a quick slash of her arm, sliced the artery in his neck that gave him life. The idiot dropped to his knees with a look of shock on his face and tried to hold his blood in with his hands. With a snarl, Finn moved to approach him, but Choden stilled him with a hand to his shoulder.

"Allow me."

The original shifter stepped to stand in front of the disgraced Alpha and placed a palm over Alastair's forehead. Choden closed his eyes a moment before glaring down at the bastard. Finn hadn't known Choden long, but he wouldn't have thought it possible for the man to emit such strong hatred and fury.

"Your crimes are too numerous and horrific to recount. Death is too kind a mercy for one such as you. I hereby curse you to never be reborn. You will spend your eternity stuck between death and rebirth, ever searching, but never attaining your material body ever again."

Choden stepped back and Alastair's now-lifeless body tumbled to the floor. Finn watched in shock as Choden dropped to his knees beside the corpse and shed a tear, which he allowed to land on the blood stained shirt Alastair wore.

"I have never before uttered a curse. This is the first time I have had to do such a thing, and I find it has stained my soul."

Finn caught the man's arm and helped him rise up as more growls and sounds of fighting came from downstairs.

"What the hell is going on down there?"

"Alastair was keeping his past mistress and her mate down there, allowing his guards to use them every night. Shelley's mate is down there too. All three were locked down."

"I freed them all when I freed Finn. I must go deal with them. Finn, help your mate free Shelley."

Finn was torn. Part of him wanted nothing more than to run to his mate and embrace her, but another part wanted to follow Choden to make sure he stayed safe.

"Do not fear for me, my friend. I am truly immortal, and have greater powers than you can conceive of."

Chapter Four

To say Brooke was in shock was an understatement. Choden was real, not just a bedtime story. Her mate had finally found her. And most importantly, Alastair was dead. It was almost too much to process at once. She stared at his body for a moment before the sounds of quiet sobbing snapped her out of her numbness.

"Shelley. Oh fuck, Shelley! I'm here. I'm going to get you out. Just hang on."

She fumbled around on the ground, trying to pick up the hair pins she'd dropped when Alastair had grabbed her, and just as she went to have another go at the lock, a strong male arm wrapped around her waist. The tingles of awareness that flowed over her had her dropping the pins once again as she gasped.

"Allow me, mate."

He kissed her bare shoulder before moving her to the side.

"Shelley? I'm going to kick in the door. Can you stand back?"

A muffled yes came through a moment before the man who was her destined mate lifted a large, booted foot and smashed the lock clean out of the frame. *Well, that was certainly faster than picking the lock.* Brooke went to charge through, but he caught her once more.

"Here, put this on. She's no doubt been through enough without wondering what happened to you just now."

Brooke looked down with a frown and blushed as she remembered she was basically half naked. She looked up to her mate and the ability to speak abandoned her. She barely noticed his freshly cut blond hair, or his baby blue eyes. Because he'd stripped his shirt off and she was left staring at the defined muscles of his chest and abs. *Bloody hell, I'd give anything to lick him.*

With a chuckle, he pulled the shirt over her head and she snapped out of her daze, and threaded her arms through the sleeves.

"Thanks."

She rushed into the room to find Shelley cowering on the floor near a bed.

"Shel? It's me, Brooke. You're free."

Her cousin just wildly shook her head and sobbed into her knees.

"No, I'll never be free. Not now. He'll put me down there with Becca. That'll be worse than this."

Brooke dropped down to kneel in front of Shelley and took her hands in her own.

"You are truly free. Alastair is dead. Come and see for yourself. He can't ever hurt you again."

Shelley lifted her tear-stained face to look up at her. "How? So many have tried."

"My mate came with Choden. He's real! The original shifter is real and he's here in this house right now sorting out Becca and Toby. Rick is down there too. Alastair lied to us. He told us when your mate came to save you that he killed him, but he didn't. He'd locked him up down in the basement. Your mate is here too, Shelley."

More tears came then and she shook her head. "He won't want me anymore. Not after what happened. Who would want someone so stained and broken?"

Brooke's eyes teared up again. She'd never cried as much in her entire life, as she had tonight. "He came to rescue you, even though he knew it was hopeless. He's your mate, sweetheart. He'll stand by your side, no matter what. You just wait, any moment now, he'll come bounding up those stairs and barge on in here."

For the first time Brooke took in Shelley's body—her completely naked body. Welts from what looked like a cane were on her legs and the sides of her torso. She guessed her back was covered too.

"Do you have any clothes in here?"

She shook her head. "He took them all away and beat me after Rick came."

Huddling into an even tighter ball, Shelley shook with her sobs. Brooke turned to face the doorway to see her mate standing guard. What had Choden called him? Finn, was it?

"Finn?"

His head instantly spun to her. "Yes, mate?"

"Could you please find something for Shelley to wear? There's nothing in here for her and she's naked."

His gaze darkened with fury when he briefly glanced at her cousin before he nodded and moved out of her sight.

"Shh, sweetheart. We'll get you something to wear, then we'll get you home to your parents."

She shook her head again. "I can't go home. I'm dirty, ruined. They won't want me."

"Oh, Shelley. They love you and have been desperate to find some way to get you free this whole time. What Alastair did to you doesn't make you dirty or ruined, it makes *him* a fucking monster."

Brooke was so far out of her element. She had no idea what else she could say to her sweet cousin in this moment, to help her move forward. She guessed it would take time to prove that everyone in the leap would surround Shelley with love and support. She couldn't imagine anyone showing her any kind of judgment. The entire leap knew what Alastair had been doing all these years.

"Shelley!"

The deep, booming voice of Rick vibrated up the stairs just as Finn returned and tossed a shirt toward Brooke. He wisely stepped back out of the room before Rick arrived. Brooke quickly pulled the large t-shirt over Shelley's head. Right as she helped Shelley get her arms through the holes Rick came barreling through the door. He was naked and had blood smears spread over his body. He looked a little thinner than Brooke remembered, but there was a glint in his eyes that told her his spirit was still intact.

"How are Toby and Becca?"

Rick shifted his focus from Shelley to Brooke when she posed the question. "They're alive. Choden is with them. I don't know if we'll be able to get either of them back, though. They've suffered so much." A grin flashed on his face for the briefest of moments. "Of course, being able to shift and rip those fuckers to shreds just now certainly helped."

Finn stepped back into the room, and catching Rick's attention, tossed the man a pair of sweatpants.

"Put these on. Will you three be okay for a little bit? I want to go check on Choden, see if he needs a hand."

Brooke smiled up at him. He was all Alpha, her mate. Taking command and making sure everyone was okay.

"We'll be fine until you get back."

Shelley continued to have a death-grip on her, or she'd have gone to her mate for a quick hug, maybe even a kiss. She watched him stride from the room before Rick sighing brought her attention back to him. He'd pulled on the pants, then come closer to them.

"Shelley? Baby?"

He dropped down a little away from them and Shelley cowered away from him, clinging to Brooke even tighter. Rick's shoulders slumped.

"Shh, Shelley. See? I told you he'd be here any moment. He's come for you, Shel. He wouldn't do that if he didn't want you anymore. C'mon, be brave just a little longer and let him hold you. He's suffered too. He's been down in the cell for days watching Becca get hurt and imagining it was you. Can you let him hold you? Maybe even let him carry you out to the car? I'm not sure I'm strong enough, and my mate is going to want to hold me. Today is the first time we've seen each other. I don't think h even knows my name yet. He got here in time to save me from truly being hurt, but not before Alastair laid his hands on me. We all need some reassurance tonight."

Something she said seemed to break through to her cousin, and with a deep breath and a wince, Shelley glanced up from where she clung to Brooke toward her mate. Slowly her body relaxed and Brooke moved to allow Rick room to lean in to stroke her face. Shelley shook against Brooke as she no doubt felt the tingles that happened whenever mates touched. That seemed to flick a switch in her and Shelley slowly moved to crawl over to Rick. Brooke didn't move a muscle as she watched her cousin approach her mate, who'd sat back with his arms open and his legs crossed. She didn't stop until she was curled in his lap like a kitten.

Brooke couldn't stop her own tears as she watched Rick curl around his mate and hold her close. With Rick to support her, she knew her cousin would come through this. But she also knew the carefree sweet girl who'd been taken into this house was not the one that was leaving. Shelley would never be the same again. And poor Becca. They'd been told she'd died trying to escape. Three months of nightly pack rapes. Brooke couldn't wrap her mind around the damage that would do to a woman's mind, body, and soul. Or to a man. She imagined it may even be worse on a man's psyche. She hoped Choden was as powerful as he claimed and could help them heal.

The last thing Finn wanted to do was to be separated from his mate after he'd finally found her. But he could see that Shelley wasn't going to release her hold on his woman any time soon, and Choden was alone down in the basement with who knows what situation. The shifter might be immortal, but Finn was sure he could still be hurt.

Keeping his senses on alert for anyone else who may be lurking in the house, he quickly made his way down the stairs, and following his instincts, he found the entrance to the basement. Walking past an opened door that was previously barred, he was left gagging at what he found.

There was blood everywhere, and body parts. He stepped over an arm and moved further into the dimly lit space.

"Choden? It's Finn."

His eyes had adjusted to the dull light and he could see chains on the walls and dirty stained mattresses on the floor. He could also see tools that could only have been used for torture and abuse. A shudder ran through him as bile rose up his throat. *Fucking bastards.*

Stepping over a dead snow leopard, he made it to where Choden was kneeling between two other snow leopards. He had a palm on the top of each of their heads as he chanted in a language Finn had never heard before. Finn stood silently behind Choden, waiting for him to finish whatever it was he was doing.

As he waited, he looked around the basement again and curled his lip in disgust. Alastair died way too quickly and easily for all his sins, although that curse Choden had laid on him would ensure he suffered for an eternity. Moving away from Choden, he quickly checked all the intact bodies for a pulse, confirming they were all dead. Three men and two beasts. He shook his head. That poor female had been raped by five men every night for at least three months, if not longer. And before that, she had Alastair abuse her nightly. And her mate had been forced to watch it happen, along with being abused himself. Finn couldn't hold back the shudder that ran through him.

When Choden finished chanting, Finn moved back to his side.

"Are they alive?"

"They breathe. Life is another matter." Choden had tears dripping from his chin. "I am unable to forgive myself for not knowing. I should not have left this leap alone for so long."

Finn rested a palm on his shoulder and gave it a squeeze. "You had no way of knowing. You said yourself Alastair used magic of some kind to block you. You've come now and we've saved lives tonight. If we had not come, another woman would be down here and my mate would be upstairs with that bastard. We saved lives. You can't take this upon yourself, Choden. You have how many leaps around the globe? You can't physically go to each one regularly, it's just not possible. And it's human nature to avoid places you know you're not welcome. You did all you could. You came as soon as you knew, and we've dealt with it."

Choden nodded before he stroked his palms over the leopards' heads before he moved to stand. "I need to take them with me back to Tibet. They have a long road of healing ahead of them, and I believe it will be best for them to do that away from here. In Tibet, they can stay in their snow leopard forms for as long as they like. There are still wild snow leopards in the area, so locals will think nothing of them if they are seen."

Finn frowned. "How are you going to get them there?"

"I do not travel as you do, my friend. I shall take them now, and return by morning. They are in a deep healing sleep and I don't expect them to wake for a number of days. My monk brothers will tend to them while I return here to help you and your mate get this leap back together."

With a small bow, Finn took a step away, to give Choden room. "What do you want me to do with the others until you return?"

"I doubt they want to remain here. Take them, if they'll go, to your mate's home. I visited earlier with Shelley's parents. They live next door to your mate's parents, and I believe you will find them waiting there for you all to return."

With another small bow, Finn left Choden to do what he needed to do to help those two poor shifters. His heart physically ached for the pair. He was still rubbing his knuckles over his chest when he entered the upstairs bedroom. A small smile stretched his lips. Shelley had released his mate and was now curled up in Rick's lap. The large man had wrapped himself around her and was rocking her gently as he whispered to her too quietly for Finn to hear the words.

A creaking floorboard had him swinging his gaze to his mate. She rose from her place on the floor and slowly began to walk towards him, looking hesitant, as though she doubted his want of her.

"My mate."

He whispered the words as he strode to her and gathered her to him, lifting her off her feet so he held all her weight. She wrapped her arms around his neck, and curled her legs around his waist. He ran a palm up her spine and tangled his fingers in her hair, pulling her head back so he could take her lips for the first time. Arousal shot through his system, demanding he take her and mark her, but he pushed the instincts down. It wasn't the time, or the place, for that. He hoped later he would find himself somewhere secluded with her and a bed, but he had duties to attend to first.

With reluctance he ended their kiss, nipping lightly at her lower lip as he pulled away.

"What is your name?"

She gifted him with the sweetest little grin. "Brooke."

"Well, my Brooke, we have some work to do before we can continue this. Choden will return by morning and find us. He suggested we all go to your parents' home. He mentioned that Shelley's parents would be there waiting for us."

She lowered her legs, sliding down his body, and he loosened his hold to allow her to stand, but he didn't completely release her. He needed to touch her, to assure himself she was really with him and unharmed.

Chapter Five

Oh wow, could her mate kiss! Still trying to get her brain to fire up, Brooke tried to make sense of what Finn had said.

"What do you mean Choden will return? I didn't hear anyone leave. And where are Becca and Toby?"

"Choden has many mysterious powers. And it didn't seem like the time to quiz him on how he was going to do what he said. But he told me he was going to take Becca and Toby back to Tibet, where they can take the time they need to heal. He's put them in a healing sleep, and once he settles them in with his monks, he'll return to help us here. I think he might be able to teleport. There's no other way he could get two giant sleeping snow leopards half way around the world without anyone noticing."

"Wow."

What else could she say? Before today, she'd believed Choden was nothing more than a bedtime story. She turned to Shelley and Rick in time to see Rick press a kiss to Shelley's forehead. She sighed, then took Finn's hand and moved over closer to them.

"Let's go home."

Rick nodded and rose easily with his mate in his arms. Shelley was nearly asleep and simply nuzzled against his chest as he began walking toward the door.

"I like his idea."

Before Brooke could ask what Finn meant, she was up in his arms and against his bare chest. With a smile, she reached up to nibble along his jawline, loving how he tasted. She kept that up until they made it outside.

"I brought my father's van. I didn't know what condition Shelley would be in, so put a mattress in the back for her."

Finn's muscles tensed around her a moment, before, with a kiss to her forehead, he placed her back on her feet.

"Probably best if you drive, love."

With a nod, she headed to retrieve the keys from where she'd stashed them earlier, behind the front wheel of the vehicle. While she did that, Finn opened the rear of the van and Rick climbed in with his now sleeping mate. Brooke opened the driver's door and got in.

A glance in the rearview mirror showed Rick carefully sitting down on the mattress with Shelley cradled against him. An unexpected shot of pain pierced through her heart and left her blinking back more tears. She prayed Shelley could heal from this, that she would be able to now live her life fully and with love, that she wouldn't let that bastard continue to control her from his grave.

She jerked when Finn ran his knuckles gently down her cheek.

"Shh, love. All will be well, you'll see. How about we get out of here?"

Wiping away the few tears that had managed to escape, she put the key in the ignition and started the van. As she drove slowly down the road away from Alastair's house of horrors, a thought occurred to her.

"What are we going to do with the house? All the bodies in it?"

"I'd like to burn the place to the ground, but I'm not sure we can do that. I'll check with Choden on what he can do about it all when he returns."

She nodded and didn't say another word for the rest of the drive to the house she lived in with her parents. Pulling up into the driveway, she found she couldn't move. What would her parents say? Would they be furious with her for being so reckless, or grateful she'd managed to free Shelley and kill Alastair?

"Oh fuck. I killed a man!"

It hit her like a freight train. She'd taken a man's life. He may have been evil and deserved it, but she'd still murdered him. In cold blood. She hadn't been defending herself when she rose up behind him and slit his throat. She buried her face in her hands and sobbed. She was as bad as he was.

"What have I done?"

A wash of cold air flowed over her before she found herself up against Finn's chest.

"Shh, love. You did what you had to. Don't you dare beat yourself up over ending that bastard's life. You've saved countless lives by ending his."

"My daughter did what? And who the hell are you?"

Her father's booming voice shook her from her pity party. Oh, shit. He was more than furious.

Gently setting Brooke on her feet, Finn stood tall in front of her, giving her his body for protection.

"I am Finlay Taylor, your daughter's mate. What Brooke did was brave and courageous. She has taken care of Alastair for good. Shall we discuss the details inside, where it's more private?"

Brooke wiped her hands over her face and stepped around her mate.

"Are Uncle Tim and Aunty Beth here?"

"What's going on?"

Her uncle shoved her father out of the doorway as he'd spoken.

"Uncle Tim, we found Shelley and Rick. We've brought them both home."

As her uncle froze in shock, she rushed to the rear of the van and opened the door. Shelley was awake and shaking her head as she clung to Rick. Brooke held her hand out to her cousin.

"Your parents are here, Shel. They love you and want to see you."

"I can't, Brooke. They'll see what I've become."

More bloody tears filled Brooke's eyes and she dashed at them.

"They'll see their strong, beautiful daughter who did what she had to do to survive a monster. Rick? Bring her out. We'll show her that, like you, her parents won't turn her away."

With a kiss to the top of Shelley's head, Rick shuffled over and exited the van with her still in his arms. She clung tighter to Rick and buried her face in his neck.

"Praise the Lord, you're both alive!"

Her aunt and mother both came barreling out past the stunned men to wrap their arms around Shelley and Rick.

"I really think we should move this inside."

Finn was glancing at the nearby houses as he closed the van's back door and took Brooke's hand.

"I think that would be a good idea."

Together they ushered everyone in the house, Brooke locking up the van on her way past.

Finn kept his arm around his mate's waist as his leopard continued to push at him to lay claim to her. He was still raw from watching that bastard maul her earlier. He'd shoved it all aside to deal with the situation, but now it was playing over and over in his mind like a bloody film reel. He'd nearly been too late.

"What the hell happened tonight?"

Brooke's father was not a happy man, and Finn really didn't have the energy to deal with him at the moment.

"Choden was with us tonight. He had to go back to Tibet with Becca and Toby, but he will return by morning. When he arrives, we'll tell you everything that happened. But it's extremely late, and I know I'm ready for bed, and I can feel Brooke is on the verge of collapse. I can only imagine how tired Shelley and Rick are. Could we all go to bed for now and pick this back up in the morning after we've all had some rest?"

"After you tell us what happened to Alastair and his guards. If any of them are out there, they'll come for us all. And they won't care that you're tired."

Finn frowned at his future father-in-law. "I thought you overheard us talking earlier. Alastair is dead, as are all his guards." He raised a palm as all four parents started asking questions. "Please, give us a few hours to rest. I only just found Brooke tonight and was nearly too late. I need some time with her."

Her father huffed out a breath but nodded. "Okay. You have until sunrise, then I'll be demanding answers. Tim? You want to take your girl and her mate next door to your place till then? Unfortunately, we don't have the room for everyone to sleep here."

Finn was sure most of what Brooke's father had said was for his benefit, not Tim's. He leaned down to whisper to his mate.

"I assume you have a room here we can use?"

"I, ah, I still live here."

He smiled at her case of nerves.

"Excellent. Lead the way, love. I need you."

She shuddered against him before she took his hand and led him to her room.

"My room is down here, while my parents' and brother's are upstairs. Means I have some privacy."

"Where is your brother? And how old is he?"

"He's over at a friend's place for the weekend, and he's two years younger than me."

Good to know. He wondered if she would let him claim her tonight?

"Um, I also have my own bathroom attached to my room. You know, if you want to clean up before we go to sleep."

He purred as he followed her into her room. "A shower sounds perfect."

He gave her room a quick glance. It was feminine, but not girly. There was no lace or overload of pink, but the room still declared clearly it belonged to a woman. Focusing back on his mate, Finn was mesmerized by her long, wavy, golden-blonde hair as she released it from the tight braid she'd had it in earlier. Then his gaze caught on her ass when she pulled his shirt over her head as she moved toward another door. Arousal shot through him, making his dick throb. With a groan, he adjusted himself and prowled after her.

Once in the small tiled space, he closed the door and pressed her back up against it. Before she could utter a word, he covered her mouth with his. He slid his hands up her arms to hold her face as he licked inside and danced his tongue with hers. She ran her palms up his bare chest and he purred into their kiss. By the time he pulled back, they were both breathing heavily.

"Let me see you, all of you."

"Turnabout is fair play."

He grinned at her sass. "Fair enough."

He leaned down to unlace his boots and pull them off in record time, as she pulled the remains of her sports bra off and let it fall into a bin under the sink. Her breasts were perfection. They would fill his hands to near overflowing, and her berry-red nipples were already tightened into little buds. His mouth watered for a taste, but when he stepped toward her she rose an eyebrow at him and pointed to his jeans.

"Yeah, yeah. I'm getting naked. Then I'm going to have my mouth on you, mate."

She giggled as she unclipped her belt and shimmed out of her own pants. He tried to ignore the missing section where Alastair had torn it away from her, but he couldn't. Kicking his own jeans aside, he dropped to his knees to examine the area the bastard had touched. He ran his fingers over a fading mark and bruise from Alastair's fingernails. Thanks to their shifter DNA, it would be completely healed within the next hour or so, but he still hated it was there to begin with. He leaned in and pressed a healing kiss to the area as he wrapped his arms around her thighs to hold her to him.

"I'm okay, Finn. It was nothing but a scratch. See? It's nearly healed already."

He opened his eyes and glared up at her face, as he rose to stand before her. "If you ever do something that reckless again, I swear I will shake you till your teeth rattle. You are not allowed to put yourself in danger like that ever again, you hear me?"

Looking up at him with a smile, she cupped his cheek in her palm. "I had to do something. I was tired of waiting for someone else to step in and end Alastair's reign of terror. Just because I'm female it doesn't make me any less alpha than you are. Best you remember that, mate. I will always do what I need to for this leap and those I care about."

With his heart feeling torn between his need to keep her from harm, and intense pride in her warrior's nature, he took her face in his palms and looked deeply into her beautiful, steel blue eyes.

"You are the perfect female for me. An alpha female to match my alpha male, but I have a feeling that same trait is going to send me out of my damn mind regularly. Just promise me you'll at least discuss any plans for recklessness with me before you run off and take action? So I can give you some back-up?"

She smiled broadly. "Now, that I can promise."

With a groan, he leaned in and kissed her solidly before he let his hands begin to wander once again. Her pale skin was like silk beneath his fingers.

"C'mon, let's get under the water. I need to wash all his dirt off me."

The very thought of anything from Alastair being on his mate's skin was enough to get him to back off so she could turn and move to the shower. For such a small bathroom, the shower stall was large. They couldn't get too wild in the space, but it was more than big enough for them both to shower together. And he would be the one to scrub that bastard's stench from her flesh. Then he'd happily replace it with his own scent.

Chapter Six

Once the water was the right temperature, Brooke turned to face her stunning mate. His short blond hair had looked freshly cut and styled earlier, but now it showed the evidence of how many times he'd run his hands through it since then. His blue eyes were piercing with their intensity. And his lips. Oh, she loved his mouth. The way he kissed her until she was a puddle at his feet.

Further down, she ran her gaze over his defined pecs and abs. The pair of notches over his hips left her drooling for a nibble. His erection stood tall and proud, a bead of liquid already on the tip. She stepped backward into the stall until she was under the spray. Watching his handsome face, she crooked her finger and he was on her in a flash.

She drove her fingers into his now-wet hair, the short blond lengths sliding easily between her fingers, as he devoured her mouth again. There would never be a time when she wouldn't want this man kissing her. His lips were soft as they pressed against hers, his tongue demanding as he delved into her mouth. She purred when he started stroking his palms over her body. Pulling from the kiss, he reached for the soap and washcloth and made fast work of cleaning her entire body. He touched and caressed every inch of her, and by the time he was through, she was a pulsing mess of arousal that could barely stay standing.

After he leaned her against the cool, tiled wall, she was too lost to her hormones to do much more than stay where he put her. When he moved to begin to quickly wash himself, she frowned a little, and threw in a pout for good measure.

"I wanted to do that."

He gave her a grin. "Next time I'll let you wash me. Right now, I need you too much."

His dick was big and jerked in his palm as he stroked himself a couple of times. She bit her lip at the thought of taking him inside her. She was a virgin and she wasn't sure how it wouldn't hurt to take such a large man within her.

"I'll be as gentle as I can, love. I don't want to ever hurt you."

Before she could answer him, he leaned in and suckled on her nipple, palming the other breast as he did. Her body had just started to cool down from him washing her, but now, it fired up again in a heartbeat.

"Hmmm."

He moved to suckle her other nipple. She shivered when he nipped it lightly with his teeth. With both her breasts now palmed in his hands, he lowered to kneel before her. With a final squeeze, he moved his hands down to her hips. When he lifted her right leg up so it was over his shoulder, she slapped her palms against the tiles to keep her balance. Her left leg bore her weight and she tensed as she realized he now had an up-close view of her lady parts.

She swallowed and licked her lips, ready to say something, anything, to get him to stop staring at her most private part like he was. But before she could think of a single word, he lightly stroked his finger down her slit, then back up to circle her clit. With a purr, she tilted her hips toward him, needing more. With a growl, he gave her what she wanted. His mouth covered her core and he began thrusting his tongue in and out of her, giving her a taste of what, she hoped, his dick would soon be doing.

Brooke couldn't wait.

She gripped his hair in her fist and held him against her as he began teasing her clit with his thumb. She couldn't believe she was already on the verge of climaxing. The coil in her lower belly was tight and ready to blow. She moaned his name and he started purring. Stars took over her vision as she trembled and ground herself against her mate's tongue. The vibration of him purring was enough to kick her over the edge and she cried out as she came apart for her mate for the first time.

When she became aware of her surroundings again, she was lying on her bed, with Finn beside her, stroking his fingers lightly over her skin.

"You are so beautiful."

"Hmmm. You're not so shabby either, my mate."

His gaze flicked up to hers. "Ah, you've come back to me. I hadn't expected that. For you to disappear from me for a little bit."

"I've never been with a male before. I have no idea what to expect."

He moved to cover her body with his, an arm on either side of her shoulders as he held himself above her. "You are the only lover I will ever know. I've never touched another before you, never wanted to. I knew you were out there waiting for me."

She stroked her fingertips over his face, learning every inch of him.

"So why did it take you five years to find me? Your accent is British, so I know you must live somewhere not too far from here."

He leaned down to kiss her before he moved to lie beside her. The moment he settled, she rolled to face him and started to trail her hands over his torso and arms. Silky flesh over rock-hard muscle. He was sex on a stick for sure. He copied her movements, caressing her breasts and flat stomach, then up over her hip and ribs to start again.

"I was raised in the north. My parents warned me of Alastair and what he did to females. I have a younger sister. She's a pretty little thing, and so innocent and sweet. When I left to search for you, my parents begged me to start my search elsewhere, for my sister's sake."

"This past year I've spent searching around the northern hemisphere. I'm not sure what exactly drew me back to England, but when I landed at Heathrow yesterday, Choden was there waiting for me. He told me my mate was in the Devon Leap and that my destiny was to be the next Alpha here. I told him I had no bloody clue how to be an Alpha of a leap, but I followed him here for you. Once he told me you were here, and what he'd heard from a woman named

Rachel, who'd fled to Australia from here, about what Alastair was doing, there was absolutely no way I was going to stay away. He couldn't tell me if you were his current mistress."

A shudder ran through Finn and he gripped her bicep tightly in his palm. "The thought of what he could be doing to you, while I wasted time looking in the wrong places for you, tore my heart out. Then to arrive last night to see him tearing your clothes off?" He shook his head and pulled Brooke in flush against him, her head resting over his heart so she could hear its strong beat. "Never again. No other will ever lay his hands on you again."

Emotion had a lump forming in her throat as she stared into the gaze of her mate. She'd been unsure how the bond worked with mates, unsure if it was an instant thing or something that grew with time. But with the way Finn spoke, it was clear he felt the same about her as she did him. Which was an almost instant love and affection, that she knew in her soul would last forever.

"Claim me, Finlay Taylor. Make me yours forever."

Jerking in shock, Finn frowned down at Brooke.

"Sorry, what did you say?"

He couldn't have heard right. Could he? In under twenty-four hours, he'd fallen completely in love with his feisty mate. Did she feel the same way about him?

"I asked you to claim me. But only if you want to."

She suddenly looked nervous and her body had tensed, as though she were preparing to bolt from the bed. And he felt like a heel for making her doubt his desire for her.

"I thought I was hoping for too much, wanting you to feel the same, but you do, don't you? Already, you feel something for me."

Her body slowly relaxed and she gifted him with a small smile.

"From the moment we touched, I knew you were meant for me. But I think what really sealed the deal was when you didn't make me promise to not be reckless. You just asked that I let you know before I act, so you can back me up. Everyone else in my life has tried to prevent me. My parents know I'll do it anyway, but they still try to stop me. You didn't."

Finn shrugged a shoulder. "Because I can understand your behavior. Attempting to extricate your cousin was somewhat insane to even try, but you put her well-being over your own in order to rescue her. That's what an Alpha should do. Doesn't mean I like it, but I understand it." His smile turned into a smirk. "Now, do you still want me to claim you tonight?"

A sassy grin crossed her face a moment before she reached down to grip his dick in her small hand that had him seeing double. "Well, I'm pretty sure it's morning now, not night. But yes, I'm sure. I want to be yours, to wear your mark and to leave mine on you."

He shuddered as she gently stroked him. "That feels so damn good. But I won't come in your hand, I need to be inside you. Are you on birth control, love?"

He wanted nothing more than to see her swollen with his child, but it needed to be her decision too. "No, I'm not. But, Finn, I'm twenty-six years old. I wouldn't mind one bit if we made a baby this morning."

He closed his eyes on a groan. "You are too good to be true, love."

He pulled her hand from his erection and moved to cover her body with his once more. She spread her legs to give him room and he settled over her, resting his hard length against her slick mound. He thrust a couple of times, loving how she trembled beneath him as he rubbed the underside of his dick back and forth over her slit and clit.

Tilting her hips up, she wrapped her arms around his neck.

"Please, Finn, stop teasing me!"

He pulled back, looking down to watch the head of his dick pressing against her slick opening. He pushed in, a little further with each small thrust. He didn't want to hurt her, but with her a virgin, he knew she would feel pain no matter how gently he went.

She moaned softly and he shifted his gaze to her face. "You don't fit. You're too big."

"I'll fit just fine, love. We were made to go together. You feel so good. Perfect."

With that, Finn slid a hand down her body and began to tease her clit. Her body jolted and he felt the rush of liquid coat his dick inside her, making it easier for him to slide a little deeper. When she started trembling, close to climax, he released her clit and leaned down to kiss her. The moment his lips touched hers, he thrust his full length deep into her. She cried out in pain, and he swallowed the sound. Hating that he'd hurt his love, he kept kissing her as he held still within her. He wouldn't move a millimeter until Brooke relaxed and told him she was okay.

After a few moments, her grip around his neck loosened slightly and she began to swivel her hips against him.

"Move, Finn. I need you to move."

His first stroke was slow and deep, and he watched her closely as he did it. When she showed no sign of being in pain, he sped up his thrusts, loving how her soft flesh parted for him, then surrounded him. He would never get enough of being inside his beautiful, feisty mate.

When he sensed she was getting close to the edge once more, he pulled all the way out of her body. Then with a growl he flipped her over, pulled Brooke up onto her knees and thrust back inside her hot, slick channel. He was going to mark her as was traditional, which meant he needed to come inside her like this, from behind. She gasped and fisted her hands in the sheet as Finn gripped her hips and thrust deeply into her, over and over again. A tingle ran down his spine and landed in his balls, drawing them up ready to deliver his seed to his mate. Leaning forward he reached around her and toyed with her clit again.

"Come for me, Brooke. Come and take me with you, right now."

He put command into his voice and she trembled as she complied. Her walls tightened around him, then pulsed as she cried out his name. His dick jerked within her and jet after jet of his seed left him, filling her womb, hopefully creating life. His mind spun at how good it felt to be emptying himself inside his one and only. The moment the last of his come left him, his right hand tingled and he pulled it away from her hip to watch in fascination as his snow leopard's claws appeared where his fingernails should be.

He slipped his left, fully human hand under her, lifting her upper body up so her back was pressed against his chest.

"Watch me, mate. Watch me mark what's mine."

She shivered and tilted her head down. With his left hand wrapped around her breast, he placed his right hand over the flesh above her right hip bone. Then he flexed his fingers down, sending his claws deep into her flesh, before he dragged them up an inch or so in an arc. The magic of the marking would mean no pain for her, but instead a rush of arousal. She purred and came again as he withdrew his claws, and his dick twitched within her, coming back to life once more, at the feel of her walls rippling around him.

"Your turn, baby."

Reluctantly Finn pulled free from her body and flipped them both so Brooke could sit above him. He knew the alpha female in her would want to control her marking of him.

The fact Finn rolled them over, giving her control of how she marked him made Brooke love him all the more. His dick lay hard against his abs, clearly ready to take her again. She was a little tender, but not enough to stop her from grabbing him with her non-clawed hand, and guiding him back within her. She purred louder at how good it felt to have him fill her so completely. He gripped her hips as his own purring joined hers to fill the air around them with the sound of two very happy felines.

"Your turn to watch, mate."

She placed her palm over his left pec, over his heart, and with him watching, Brooke dug her claws in and dragged them down an inch or so before pulling them free. The moment her claws were out of his flesh, Finn thrust up deep within her and came. She could feel his dick jerk as he filled her again with his seed. *Please let me get pregnant from this.* Nothing could make this claiming more perfect other than them creating a life from it.

When he finished climaxing, he tugged her down so she lay over him, her face landing beside her mark on him. She lightly ran her fingers over it, smiling when he started purring again. Four wide scratch marks revealed his snow leopard spots. She had the same mark over her hip bone now. Any human that saw either one would think it was nothing more than a tattoo, but any shifter who saw them would know instantly that the shifter was mated.

"I hope for that too."

Her breath caught. "Hope for what?"

"That we created life tonight. I caught your thought through our bond."

She smiled against his chest. "That could take some getting used to. I don't know you'll want to be inside my head all the time."

He chuckled. "Well, it will help me work out when you're about to do something reckless before you do it."

Brooke nuzzled her face against his mark before she slipped to his side. Finn shuddered when his spent dick slid from her body, then curled his arm tightly around her when she wriggled up against his side. She wrapped a leg over his, rubbing her mound against his hip bone in the process, earning her a low growl.

"Keep that up, and I'll have to take you again."

A yawn stopped her from answering right away. "Maybe later. Need to sleep now."

Finn chuckled and kissed the top of her head. "Sleep, my mate. I promise I'll be waking you up for more later."

Unfortunately, when she woke hours later, it wasn't because Finn was fulfilling his promise. Nope, it was to her father pounding on her door.

"The sun is up, and you two have some explaining to do. Get your butts out of bed and get out here."

Brooke groaned, then stretched.

"There goes my plans for the morning then."

Her cheeks heated as she considered what he must think of her. She was twenty-six years old and still living at home.

"Sorry. We'll start looking for our own place today. I didn't want to risk living alone with Alastair as Alpha. Not that living at home would have stopped him if he'd really wanted to take me."

He rolled toward her and kissed her firmly. "You don't need to be embarrassed about living with your parents. I'm glad you chose to stay here, where you knew it was safest for you. We'll find our own place soon enough."

With that, Finn hopped up and strode over to her bathroom. She sat in shock for a minute, her gaze glued to her mate's very fine ass as he moved. Brooke couldn't believe he didn't have an issue with her still living at home.

"Where do you live?"

He stopped in the doorway and glanced over his shoulder, smirking when her cheeks heated once more. Dammit, she could ogle her mate's butt if she wanted to.

"Like what you see, love?"

She gave him a cheeky grin. "Sure do, and it's all mine."

He chuckled and leaned one hand against the doorframe after he turned to give her a full frontal view. *Very nice, indeed.*

"I've been living out of my bag for the past year, but before that I lived with my parents and sister. I had no reason to leave and their house was big enough for all of us."

"They didn't mind?"

Her parents had their moments where they'd wanted her and her brother to move out. Brooke suspected it was mainly due to how she and her brother cramped their sex life by living in the same house as them.

"We live in a large farmhouse. Big enough we all have plenty of space to ourselves, and they knew once I found my mate, I'd be moving out. My sister is only nineteen, so she'll be living there a few more years yet, anyway."

With a nod, she climbed out of bed.

"C'mon, we better get cleaned up fast before Dad comes in here with a bucket of cold water to throw at us."

It certainly wouldn't be the first time he'd decided to wake her up that way, if he did.

Chapter Seven

Half an hour later Finn found himself standing in Brooke's family's lounge room. He still hadn't learned her parents' names. He really should get that information soon. His hand was entwined with Brooke's as she stood next to him. He was wearing the same jeans as he had the previous night and was still shirtless, as he needed to go back to Alastair's to get his car where he'd left his bag of clothes. He supposed he could have worn the shirt that he'd given Brooke yesterday, but she'd stashed it away somewhere in her room. No way did he want to ask for it back—he loved that she wanted to keep it for herself, even if he didn't have a clue why she'd want to.

Another bonus was that this way, his mating mark was well and truly on display. Not that he didn't think the whole house wouldn't have heard what they got up to earlier this morning. When they'd first entered the room, Brooke's mother had taken one look at his mark and teared up. With a beaming smile she'd hugged her daughter tightly to her, then him. Her father, on the other hand, had stood back frowning. He still was.

A knock on the door had them all turning in that direction. Brooke's father rushed over to beat her mother to answer it. Finn figured her mother was where Brooke got her reckless streak from. While they were both out of the room, he turned to Brooke.

"What are your parents' names, love?"

"Peter and Dawn. Who do you think is at the door? Do you think Alastair had more guards?"

He gave her a quick kiss. "They wouldn't have knocked, love. Hopefully it's Choden returning."

Sure enough, a few moments later Choden entered the room, along with Rick, Shelley and Shelley's parents. Choden greeted both Peter and Dawn before he made his way over to Finn and Brooke.

"It gives me great joy to see you have completed your mating. Congratulations."

"How are Becca and Toby?" Brooke's voice sounded strained and Finn kicked himself for not giving her all the information he knew about the pair.

"They are currently in their animal forms, in a deep, healing sleep. I do not expect them to wake for a number of days. I vow I will let you know of any progress they make as time passes."

Peter stepped to the center of the room and cleared his throat. "Can someone please explain what happened last night?"

Choden turned to face Peter. "I would suggest you all have a seat before I begin to explain."

Finn followed his mate to the couch, where he pulled her onto his lap.

"There's not enough room if we all sit next to each other." He whispered into her ear when she tried to move to his side.

Rick followed his lead and sat beside them on the loveseat, and nestled Shelley on his lap. The poor female still looked beyond tired and worn down. Brooke reached out a hand toward her cousin, who took it tightly in her grip. Finn and Rick both shifted their mates, so they could comfortably maintain the contact.

"I spoke with the elder four of you yesterday about Alastair and what he has been doing. You were not the only families I visited." Choden frowned. "It took me longer than I had expected to visit with everyone I needed to before I could return to Finn. Once I rejoined Finn, we made our way directly to Alastair's home. We found the rear door open and the house in darkness. As we made our way inside, we could hear the sounds of several men enjoying themselves in the basement, and the moans of a female."

Choden paused to shake his head and sigh heavily. The poor shifter was still carrying so much guilt over the fact he hadn't come sooner. "A sound from upstairs alerted us to Alastair's presence and Finn rushed up toward the sound. He found his mate, our brave but reckless Brooke, who had been on her own rescue mission. However, Alastair had caught her."

Finn tightened his hold on Brooke, snarling at the memory.

"Calm yourself, Alpha. It is done."

Choden's words had him swallowing his emotions. He took a couple deep breaths before pressing a kiss to his mate's temple. "I'm sorry for interrupting, Choden."

Choden bowed slightly before he continued. "Alastair had Brooke locked down and had begun to undress her. When I arrived, it was to discover Finn had also been locked down. I removed that particular ability from Alastair, which, in turn, freed all he had been using the ability on." Choden smiled gently at Brooke. "Finn lunged for Alastair but before he could reach him, Brooke pulled a knife and slit his throat.

"I then left them to free Shelley while I went to the basement to see what his guards had been up to." Choden's body shuddered. "He had Rick, Toby and Becca locked in the basement." He glanced to Rick, who nodded for him to continue. "At nightfall each night, he would lock down all three of them, then at nine he would dismiss his guards from their duties and they were then free to go use Becca however they pleased."

Brooke tightened her grip on her cousin and him. Her tears wet his shoulder where her head now lay. The two older women began sobbing and the men cursed. Finn didn't miss the fact Choden was omitting the abuse Toby had suffered. He had no issue with that. The entire leap didn't need to know the full extent of what happened in that house. And if he were in Toby's shoes, he wouldn't want them knowing.

"When I removed the lockdown, the three of them shifted and killed the guards. All five of them. Three bodies were human while two were snow leopard. When I entered the basement, the three turned on me and I was forced to lock them down again for all our safety." Choden looked up around at them all. "That is the real reason Alpha's have that ability. For safety purposes in life or death situations.

"I first went to Rick and was able to heal all his physical, and ease some emotional, wounds. I freed him and he shifted to human. Once he realized who I was, and that I posed no danger to him or his friends, he ran from the basement in search of his mate."

"Toby and Becca were a different story. Their wounds were deep, Becca even more so than Toby. I have put them both in a healing sleep, which, as I said, they will stay in for at least the next few days. They are being cared for by my monk brothers in Tibet and are perfectly safe. I have no idea if, or when, they will return to England. Only time will reveal what their new destinies will be."

"Where was our Shelley in all of this?"

"Brooke? Would you care to tell that part of things?"

Finn was extra grateful she was sitting on his lap when she nuzzled her face against his mating mark. His dick stiffened instantly into a hard, aching erection. Seemingly oblivious to the reaction she caused, Brooke moved to sit upright and face the others. While she maintained her hold on her cousin, she wiped her eyes with her other hand.

"After Choden went down to the basement, Finn kicked out the lock on Shelley's door and I went in. Well, Finn actually gave me his shirt to cover up with first. Shelley was trying to hide beside the bed. I went to her and after some coaxing, got her to believe me that Alastair was dead. Finn went and found a shirt for her to dress in. Then, when Rick arrived, it took a little more convincing before she'd allow him near her. From there, we all left the house and came here."

By the way Brooke spoke just the bare facts, Finn knew she'd left out a lot of what had been said and done in that room for Shelley's sake. He also believed that was why Choden allowed her to choose what was said publicly of the rescue. Finn was certain with all Choden's powers, he knew precisely what had taken place in that room, and how awesome his mate was to have accomplished so much with her cousin in such a short time. He remembered the cowering, trembling woman he'd glimpsed when he'd first kicked down the door, remembered her saying she was too broken for anyone to want anymore.

He looked over to her now. She was still pale and had dark circles under her eyes, but Shelley appeared comfortable sitting on her mate's lap. As Choden had spoken, both her parents had moved to stand near her, her mother laying a hand on her back. Shelley hadn't pulled away from the contact, which considering how fearful she was to even see them earlier, had Finn amazed. And hopeful that the female would make a fast and full recovery from her time with that monster.

Having said what happened as concisely as possible, Brooke wanted to take the pressure off her cousin before the others started with any questions. So, she turned to Choden.

"What do we do with his house? And the bodies?"

"After we finish here, I will go and dispose of the entire building. The evil in that place has seeped into the very stones within its walls."

She really wanted to ask how he'd do that, but respect for the original shifter had her biting her tongue.

"Who will lead our leap now? Are you going to do it?"

Choden smiled at her father's question. "No, I will never directly lead any leap. Finn and Brooke are your new Alpha couple. They are both strong Alphas and will do well with piecing the Devon Leap back together. Unlike Alastair, they both understand that we are here to protect, not to harm. It was why we were created, and why we continue to exist in the world. To protect."

Brooke recalled hearing the story of their race's creation as a child, but she couldn't recall all the details.

"Choden? Could you tell us the story of our creation?"

The original shifter relaxed into his seat, as if he appreciated her requesting he tell a story that was happy in nature after he was forced to deal with so much evil.

"Of course, my dear girl. I haven't had the pleasure of telling it myself for quite some time. In the year 1759, when I was just a boy of fifteen, I was living in a monastery high in the Tibetan mountains. Near the monastery, a leap of snow leopards lived. They regularly came to visit us, and us them, so when we noticed their rapidly declining numbers, we grew concerned. My mentor and I discovered a powerful spell that would combine a beast with a man. We believed such a creature would be better able to keep the leap protected from human poachers than pure animals.

"I was particularly close with one of the snow leopards, so I offered myself and him up when the time came to conduct the magic. The spell was cast as the moon rose and it worked perfectly. My body, mind, heart and soul were combined with that of the animal. And I was able to locate the hunters illegally hunting the snow leopards and put a stop to their actions.

"It was not until years later that we realized the spell was more powerful than we anticipated. You see, Halley's Comet had been passing over our heads when the spell was cast, and it had amplified and connected with the magic. Instead of just myself being turned into a shifter, a mated pair was conceived on each of the seven continents that night. Fifteen years later, these people all turned into snow leopards when the moon rose on the night of their birthday. When we started hearing stories of snow leopards being in places they shouldn't have been, we went to investigate and found more shifters. Even now, every time the comet passes over Earth, another seven pairs of shifters are conceived and it is up to all of us to keep our eyes and ears open for signs of them."

Her father shook his head. "How does one as evil as Alastair come from a race designed to protect?"

A heavy sigh left Choden. "I believe when his mate passed, it left him empty and very angry. That anger turned to bitterness that became evil. He allowed himself to be eaten up by it. I can honestly say, in my nearly three hundred years on this Earth, I have never seen a shifter such as he. And I hope to never see another."

"What's to stop any Alpha from doing what Alastair did? This power they have to lock other shifters down is dangerous."

Choden gave her father a gentle smile, like one a parent gives a child when they're not understanding a simple concept. Brooke hid her grin against Finn's chest.

"Most Alphas go their entire lives without using that particular ability. It is there so an Alpha can protect his shifters from doing something that will get them injured or killed. For example, the Tasmanian Leap's previous Alpha used it to prevent one of his men from running straight into a trap set by Trigger. It, no doubt, saved the man's life."

Brooke sensed there was more to that story but Choden didn't look like he was going to share any more details. And as curious as she was about the Tasmanian leap, she was more curious about who, or what, the hell Trigger was.

"Who, or what, is Trigger?"

A smile tugged at her lips when her mate voiced the question she was thinking.

"My guess is with your leap here so scattered, and with so many trying to stay hidden from Alastair, you have also remained hidden from Trigger. That will change. Trigger are our enemies, an organization that hides behind a research company. They are out to destroy our race completely. They are vicious and nasty, and will not hesitate to harm any shifter they find. Whether they be man, woman or child, they do not care. I have seen them take out entire leaps, leaving none behind. Finn, you and Brooke will need to be on constant lookout for signs of them. Many of their hunters have their logo tattooed on them. It is a symbol that looks somewhere between a cat's eye and the trigger from a rifle. If you look on the internet for Trigger Corporation, you will find their public front and pictures of their logo."

Finn stiffened beneath her. "Choden, I'm not ready for any of this. To be Alpha of an entire leap."

Choden waved off his concerns. "Sure you are. Call your parents, they will come to help, as will Brooke's and Shelley's parents. I will call Dominic tomorrow and put the two of you in touch. He is the Alpha closest in age to yourself. I am certain that in no time you will have this leap thriving once more. Trigger are a threat, but they can be handled. I will stay another day or so to help you, but then I must go to attend to Toby and Becca."

Brooke kissed her mate on his cheek.

"You'll do fine, love."

She mentally added that compared to what Alastair had done, anything Finn did would be an improvement.

Epilogue

Four months later

"You reckon he can teleport?"

Finn tapped his fingers against the table as he waited for Dominic, the Alpha of the Tasmanian Leap to answer his question.

"Not sure, mate. But if it's not teleportation, it's something similar. I mean he left here not more than an hour ago and you're expecting him on your doorstep any moment. No airline is that bloody fast."

"Maybe I'll try to follow him next time he leaves here. See if I can witness how he travels."

Dominic laughed. "Good one. He'd know you were there, guarantee it. You'll just need to accept that the man is a mystery and move on. We all have to at some point. Tell me, how are things going over there now?"

Finn sighed. He knew he needed to stop analyzing Choden's abilities. It was just a nice distraction from his more serious tasks.

"The older folk are finally backing me. Choden helped a lot with that. Some of them were just flatly refusing to accept an Alpha under the age of forty." He chuckled. "The younger women have all but formed a fan club for Brooke."

Dominic chuckled along with him. "The female did kill Alastair. She's fully earned the right to be labeled a badass. There's nothing quite like an alpha female. You'll have to bring your mate over here sometime, then you can both meet my Adele."

Finn glanced out the window to his own mate, who sat rocking slightly on the chair he'd put out on their back deck so she could do just what she was doing right now. She had her palm on her swollen belly, rubbing it in slow circles.

A wide grin spread over his face.

"That sounds great. Hopefully in another couple of months things here will have settled down enough Brooke and I can come over."

"I'd offer for us to come to you, but my brother's mate is going to drop her bundle of joy any day now. Tina would help my mother string me up if I was halfway around the world when the big day finally arrives."

Finn chuckled again. He loved listening to Dominic tell him tales of all his leap brothers and sisters. He'd told Finn how Conner, his blood brother, found his mate living in a twisted version of Cinderella. But the one who always caught his attention most was the man's adopted daughter, Kelly. She'd been held captive along with her mother. Her tormentor had murdered her mother, then moved on to physically abusing the young girl. The fact she seemed to be living a normal life now, just a few years later, gave Finn hope that Shelley would be okay.

"How's Kelly doing?"

"Good. She went backward a bit in her recovery when we lost my father, but she's back on track now. My Mum has been tutoring her so she's almost caught up to her peers at school. Conner bought her some art supplies a while back now and she's really taken to that. I assume you're thinking of Shelley?"

"Yeah, she's doing better, but so many things still set her off."

"PTSD isn't just for soldiers, mate. A lot of abuse victims suffer from it too. If you haven't already, you need to find her a shifter counselor. If you can't find one locally over there, we have a great one here that I'm sure we could work out a video link with, if you need it."

Finn scrubbed a palm over his hair. "It's been a struggle to find one. We can hardly go to a human doctor and explain what she went through. The video link thing might be worth trying."

"I'll get Jennifer to call you. She's an older shifter and fully qualified. I'll tell her what happened so Shelley won't have to."

"That would be great. Thank you."

"No problem at all. Now, I'm going to have to leave you. I need to go read a story to Kelly before she goes to bed. Kid might be a teenager, but she still loves being read to."

Finn smiled. The time difference always threw him off. It was early morning here in England.

"Yeah, well, I guess because she never had it as a kid, she appreciates it now. I'll let you go do your thing. Thanks for the call, and we'll chat again soon."

"Shall do. Remember, you can call me whenever you need to. Now, you go enjoy some time with that mate of yours."

He hung up and quietly moved over to the window to watch his beautiful mate for a few moments. The pregnancy had her glowing. Thankfully her morning sickness had cleared up in the past two weeks so she could actually enjoy being pregnant now.

Watching her mouth move as she spoke to their unborn baby had his heart aching. He rubbed a fist over his chest. How had he gotten so lucky? A beautiful mate he adored, and who loved him back. And a son on the way. When Choden bailed him up at the airport that day not so long ago, he'd never have thought he'd end up here. But he was eternally grateful he had.

Rubbing her palm over her swollen belly, Brooke looked out over the ocean, as her unborn child thrived within the safety of her womb. She adored this house that Finn had found for them. It was out of town a little, up near the cliffs, so she could stare out at the waves and relax whenever she needed to.

"How's my beautiful mate this morning?"

She lifted her face with a smile as Finn lowered his lips to hers. As he kissed her good morning, his palm joined hers in caressing her rounded belly.

"I'm doing okay. Your son was up most of the night doing aerobics, so I think I'll stay home and have a quiet one today."

Finn smirked at her. "So he's already mine when he's being naughty, huh?"

"Naturally. That's how it always works Where are you off to today?"

"Choden will be here any moment to join me in searching for more of the scattered shifters. Neither of us wants any shifter left out in the cold, now that the leap is back on its feet."

That it was. True to his word Choden had leveled Alastair's home. In its place was now a beautiful garden. No one had wanted to risk building another house on the land, just in case whatever magic that monster had used was strong enough to haunt the next home. Those shifters that had remained living in and around Lynton had quickly joined Brooke and Finn in rebuilding their leap. They'd all missed the old days, when the leap would gather together and enjoy each other's company. It was a slow process getting some of the more removed members to rejoin the leap, and no one was being forced. Brooke was confident over time their leap would flourish into something as beautiful as it had once been.

"Has Choden mentioned how Becca and Toby are doing?"

Her mate, and husband, lowered to sit beside her and lifted her feet onto his lap, where he started to massage them.

"They both continue to prefer to be in their snow leopard form. Choden mentioned they have bonded with the local leap of wild snow leopards and seem content to live their lives with them. I don't think they'll ever come back to England, and honestly, I can't blame them."

Her heart ached for the pair of them. The guards hadn't just used Becca, but Toby too. Along with Choden and Rick, she and Finn had decided to never say a word of that, not wanting information to get out in case the pair did decide to return one day. Alastair's evilness was deeper than any of them had realized. Rick had been spared from the rapes, but he'd known it would happen at some point. The guards had teased him that as soon as Alastair gave the go-ahead they would be all over him. A shudder ran through her. The horror and fear all four of them had lived through in that house was beyond comprehension.

"No, I don't think I'd want to come back either if I were them. Rick and Shelley are coming over later this afternoon. Do you think you'll be back by then?"

Shelley was slowly but steadily healing under the care and love of her mate and family. Every now and then something would trigger a memory, and she'd retreat into herself. But that was occurring less and less as time passed.

"I'll do my best, but I can't promise anything. I honestly don't know where Choden intends to lead me today."

Brooke smiled. The original shifter had told them quite a bit, but he was still pretty much a mystery to them all. Her mate might well be gone for days. But she didn't complain, she was simply grateful that Choden continued to come back to help them. They'd have been in a hell of a mess if he hadn't, especially in the beginning.

Due to Finn's young age, a lot of the older shifters took some time to accept him as their new Alpha. But Choden made sure they all saw how strong and fair he was, so it thankfully hadn't taken long for Finn to be respected by the leap. Of course, all the young ones thought she was some kind of superhero for killing Alastair.

Finn chuckled at her. "You are a badass alpha female for sure."

She pouted at her mate. "You eavesdropping on my thoughts again, my mate?"

"I only heard that last part. You were thinking it pretty loud, I couldn't miss it."

Brooke shook her head then reached her arms over to her sexy mate. Following her lead, he pulled her onto his lap. Then, with his hands tangled in her hair, he took possession of her mouth in the way she loved. Her toes curled and her whole body melted against him as wave after wave of arousal flowed over her.

When the need to breathe had her pulling back, she nibbled her way across his jaw.

"I love you, Finlay Taylor and I'm so grateful fate gave me such a wonderful mate to spend my life with."

Her mate's expression softened to one of absolute adoration, making her heart swell even more with love for him. "And I love you, Brooke Taylor. Fate truly did bless us both by pairing us as mates. I couldn't ask for a more perfect one. And I know you're going to be a wonderful mother to our little gymnast."

A sense of peace and warmth spread from her heart to every part of her body, and with a huge grin, Brooke nestled herself down into her mate's embrace, making the most of having him all to herself for a little while longer before he went out for the day. His large palm returned to her belly caressing their unborn son.

She couldn't have asked for more.

The End

Continue the Fire and Snow Series by going back to the beginning and getting to know Dominic and his mate, Adele, in Guardian's Heart.
Turn the page to discover more about the series and to get a taste from Guardian's Heart.

www.khloewren.com/FireAndSnow

Other Fire and Snow books:

More books to come.

Out Now:

Guardian's Heart

Fire and Snow: Book One

The last thing Snow Leopard Shifter Dominic expects to find at an accident scene is his mate, the beautiful Adele. But after four years of dreaming of her, there she is, right in front of him. However, winning the heart of his lonely, grieving mate is no simple task. Just as their relationship begins to heat up, a gravely injured child, Kelly, stumbles into their lives after escaping and fleeing her abuser. Will Dominic and Adele's bond grow stronger as they nurture and protect Kelly? Will their relationship be able to survive all that fate plans on throwing their way?

Noble Guardian

Fire and Snow: Book Two

After watching his older brother win the heart of his mate, Conner White can't wait for his turn. When he finally has his first dream of his mate, he is both relieved that he knows who she is and worried as he hasn't been able to get near her since he caught a glimpse of her at his brother's wedding weeks earlier.

Tina Anderson is beyond miserable. Her mother abandoned her after a life altering injury that left the vibrant gymnast in a wheelchair. Her father has been forced to leave her to go work off shore. She's been left in the care of a harsh bitter woman who is only after her father and will do whatever she deems necessary to take her place in his life. No matter the cost.

Conner and Tina's road to happiness is filled with twists, turns and pot holes, but are they strong enough to pull each other through it all?

Guardian's Shadow

Fire and Snow: Book Three

Jessie loves his life as a carefree rally driver, until a chance meeting with a sexy red haired firefighter changes everything. As a Comet Shifter, Jessie's never met another Snow Leopard shifter before finding Kit, the woman who's haunted his dreams for the past five years.

Kit's one tough female. She's been keeping herself busy protecting those she cares for but deep inside she craves her mate. When her path finally crosses with Jessie sparks fly … and they aren't all the good kind!

Just as they begin to get along, Kit's dark secret is revealed, and it's not only Jessie and Kit that will be put to the test in the aftermath.

Fierce Guardian

Fire and Snow: Book Four

He's found his true mate at last-but she's caught in a deadly trap.

Australian Xander Moore is one of a secret cadre of humans who can shift into the form of a snow leopard. His predator side is gorgeous and deadly. He's also lonely. Somewhere out there is his true mate ... if he can find her before the Triggers destroy them all.

To the team he leads in search of the brutal Triggers, Xander is known for his calm strength in the midst of danger. But when he glimpses the mate he's dreamt of for years, he's torn between the mission and his instinctive drive to protect and claim. Xander loses focus, leading to dire consequences.

British visitor Rachel Bell is caught in a trap. Her boyfriend's offer of a job to extend her visa has turned into forced servitude in his bar. The night he beats her and locks her in their apartment, she's desperate enough to get help the only way she can-by starting a fire.

When her abuser attacks her brave rescuers, Rachel discovers she herself may be a deadly weapon. Is she brave enough to unleash her shocking new abilities and save them all?

A taste of
Guardian's Heart

Prologue

Rosebery, Tasmania, Australia
November 2007

Conner let loose a low whistle as Dominic walked into the station house kitchen.

"Damn, you look like shit, Dom, why don't you go crash out back for a bit? I'll come get you if we get called out."

"Thanks, little brother, so feeling the love right now."

Dominic said in a voice heavy with sarcasm as he strode over to the coffee machine. Conner leaned back on his seat, taking a sip from his own caffeine fix. He furrowed his brow as he took in the sight of his older brother. Dominic wasn't standing tall and proud like he did ordinarily, instead, he appeared to be inches shorter than his actual six foot six height with the way his shoulders were slumped and his head hung down. His short black hair, normally clean and neat, looked greasy like it was at least a few days overdue for a wash and his face had, Conner guessed, at least a couple of days' worth of beard growth roughening it.

Conner and his only brother had always been extremely close. They could read each other's moods and body language so well that often it appeared to others that they could communicate telepathically. A very handy skill set when they were out fighting fires. It also meant it hadn't slipped his notice that over the last few days Dominic had been getting worse, looking more wrecked each day. He was worried about his big bro, both on a personal level and a professional one. With summer and the bushfire season just around the corner, none of them could afford to be off their game. Conner placed his can of Coke on the table as Dominic sat across from him and took a long drag of his coffee with his eyes closed.

"I'm serious, Dom, something's up. Has been for a couple days. You gonna spill? Or do I have to sic Dad onto you?"

"Yeah right, like to see you try pulling that one off."

Dominic chucked as he'd spoken but it wasn't long before his brother's features grew serious—finally, they were making some progress.

"They're just dreams, Conner. I'm fine."

Conner wasn't fooled by his brother shrugging his shoulder or by his casual tone.

"Bullshit you're fine. What dreams?"

"My mate turned twenty-one about six weeks ago."

Bloody hell! Conner held Dominic's stare as shock pinged around his skull.

"You're dreaming of your mate already? You only turned twenty-one eight months ago. But hang on, why has it got you so stressed out? I thought once you started dreaming of your mate, life is all sunshine and lollipops or some shit? Did you meet her and stuff it up or something?"

Lifting his can to take a drink, Conner recalled an earlier conversation with their father. One about the shifter's version of the birds and the bees. Their father had explained to them how when a male shifter's mate turns twenty-one, he would start seeing her face in their dreams. As time goes by the nightly visions reveal what she looks like from head to toe and, if after a decade or so the male still hadn't found her, he would begin to see places, people and things that she holds dear. Basically, the dreams provided a male with all the information he needed to go searching for his mate, the longer he took to find her, the more facts he received to assist him. Although, generally speaking, fate put mates in each other's path long before a male needed to go actively searching for her.

"Six weeks ago when they began, it was beyond amazing. After the first dream I felt so alive and had a buzz in my system, you know how it feels after you go for a good solid run? Like that, but twenty-four/seven. And at night, every night, she's all I see. She's so damn beautiful..."

By the glazed look in Dominic's eyes, Conner guessed he'd lost him to memories of his dreams, which wasn't going to help him work out what was wrong. It was time to pull Dominic back to reality. Conner cleared his throat and hoped his voice would stay steady.

"Yeah, yeah, don't need my nose rubbed in it. So what changed?"

"I'm not sure, it's like—damn it—I think she's in trouble or in pain, but I don't know how to find her. I've never seen her outside my dreams and it's still too early for me to see anything other than her. I just don't know where to start or what to do." Dominic scrubbed his hands over his face on a sigh.

Conner's gut churned as he fought the jealousy rising within him. He didn't want to feel like this. He knew he had most likely years until he would dream of his mate, it made sense that his elder brother would find his mate first, but his emotions weren't listening to logic.

"Have you spoken to Dad about it? I'm pretty sure he'd have some advice for you. He did tell us to let him know when we started dreaming of our mate."

"Nah, I haven't. He has his hands full at the moment, you know that. With fire season around the corner, he's flat out getting everything ready, and then there's The Search; I mean, hell, they've only found three pairs globally. That means there are still four pairs out there, including one in Australia. They all would have got the shock of their lives on their fifteenth birthdays in 2001 when they suddenly shifted to snow leopards at nightfall don't you think? It's important that we find them before they lose their minds.

Six years not knowing what is going on is a long time. That's more important than my mate issues."

Conner rolled his eyes, he couldn't help it. Dominic was being a coward, looking for excuses so he didn't have to admit weakness to their father.

"Bullshit, bro—you're scared, that's all. You know as well as I do that Dad is *never* too busy for family. Hell, he's never too busy to help anyone who needs it, and he manages to multitask just fine. He'll be pissed if you don't go to him for help when he finds out you needed it."

Shaking his head in resignation, Conner got up and using every ounce of his supernatural strength, he hauled his brother's butt out of his chair. Dominic might be older, but Conner had more muscle. Before Dominic could come to his senses and stop him, he had him half way out the door. Pulling his arm free, Dominic growled at him.

"What the hell, Conner?"

"You need to go ask Dad for advice, and I want to hear what he has to say, so I'm coming along."

With a sigh, Dominic allowed Conner to usher him down the hall and into their father's office. He hated when his brother saw through his defense mechanisms and made him deal with things when he just wanted to hide. Hiding was good. Safe. He knew he should have told his dad when the dreams first started. It was, after all, what his father had asked them to do and Dominic had been meaning to tell him. It's just that other things kept happening and he hadn't got around to it yet.

His dad looked up from his desk, cocking an eyebrow when he saw them enter. Dominic was sure the sight of his nineteen-year-old, six foot two son, trying to muscle his twenty-one year old, six foot six son through the door would keep his dad chuckling for some time. Despite the fact Dominic wasn't in the mood for humor, he could see how others would think the image they made looked funny as hell. He would if he were watching it.

"What can I help you boys with?" he asked in a voice laced with more than a touch of humor.

Before Dominic could speak, Conner spoke up.

"Dom has something he needs to discuss with you."

The smirk dropped off Conner's face when their father turned his full attention to him.

"So you're here because…?" their father queried with a raised eyebrow.

"I, ah, I'd really like to hear your answer, Dad."

Conner almost sounded sheepish. It was so unlike his normally confident brother that Dominic found himself biting back a chuckle. He understood where his brother was coming from; he'd want to know too if he were in Conner's position.

"Alrighty then, you've got my curiosity spiked. What's up, Dominic?"

Dominic shut the door then dragged himself over to sit in the couch near his dad's desk. Conner dropped down next to him.

"Well, I've started dreaming of my mate…" Dominic proceeded to tell his dad about his dreams and how they'd recently changed.

"Hmm, that explains it. Your mother and I had been wondering about what's been eating at you lately." He paused to scrub his hand over his face. "I haven't been as diligent in making either of you aware of our ways, have I? For that I am sorry."

He got up from his desk and came around to sit in the chair next to the couch.

"So, you boys are curious about mating and all it entails? Hmm, where to start…do you boys remember what I told you about the dreams starting when your mate turns twenty-one, and that you'll see more as time goes on?"

Dominic gave a quick nod as Conner sat forward and rested his elbows on his knees. Thanks to that little snippet of information, every night after he'd turned twenty-one, he'd gone to sleep with his stomach in knots of anticipation until he'd finally dreamed of her sweet face.

"Okay, I guess we'll start there then. As Dominic has found out, you are linked with your mate on an emotional level. Her pain will become yours. Now, I'm not talking about her stubbing her toe or crying over spilled milk, but when she truly suffers, like the loss of someone close, a major car crash that leaves her severely injured, that kind of thing, you'll know about it."

Angry heat rolled through Dominic. So, he had no way of finding his mate but would know when she was hurting…that was plain cruel.

"But, Dad, what good does it do me to be able to feel her pain but be unable to do a damn thing about it?" Dominic could hear the frustration in his own voice and wasn't surprised when his father glared at him.

"Don't get yourself so worked up, Dominic. There is a way that you can possibly help her. It's called Dream Bonding. You can use your shifter magic to appear in her dreams, or pull her into yours, but you must be careful; it is just as easy to do or say the wrong thing in a dream as it is in real life. Leave a bad impression in her dreams, she'll shy away from you outside of them."

Right. Visit dream. Stay quiet. Got it, he could *so* do that. A kernel of hope lit up inside his heart as he leaned forward in his seat.

"How exactly does it work?"

His mind stilled and the churning in his stomach settled. He instinctively knew if he could just see her and touch her, offer her some comfort—even if it was just in a dream—it would ease both of them.

"As you're drifting off to sleep you need to focus on her, forming a connection with her subconscious. When she's asleep, you'll find it's easy to link together. Once linked, you can either push yourself into her dream or pull her into yours. But, be aware that she will think it is just like any other dream, that it is hers alone and formed from her imagination."

Taking a deep breath, Dominic ran the process through in his mind. It sounded easy enough. He hoped like hell it worked. Frowning, he wondered what he'd do if it didn't.

The fact his mate was hurting and he wasn't with her to fix it, ate at him. His dad cleared his throat, grabbing his attention. There was more? He'd thought his dad was done.

"While we're discussing mating, I may as well educate you on other areas. Like the Marking."

With that one word, his father had Dominic's full attention. He had seen his dad's mark before but his parents had never explained how it got there, and he was definitely curious.

"Now, obviously it has something to do with sex. I'm going to skip over the 'birds and bees' part of things because I'm pretty sure you boys know all you need to know about what goes where and what can happen as a result. So, when you are inside your mate, and you both climax at the same time, your right hand will partially shift. Only your right hand.

"Your claws will sprout from your fingertips. Once your claws are fully extended, you need to scratch your mate. Now, don't worry about hurting her, it uses shifter magic so you are not cutting into her. You can leave your mark anywhere on her body but traditionally speaking, mating happens with the male taking his mate from behind and leaving his mark here." He paused to place his palm inside his right hipbone. "Once you scratch her, you need to place your palm over your mark until the magic cools. For a minute or so, you'll feel the heat radiating from the mark. Your magic will then flow through to your mate. It doesn't matter if she's wholly human or one of us, she will still sprout claws on her right hand. Like you, it will only happen to her right hand.

"At that point, you need to leave her body so you can turn her to face you. Placing her hand over your heart, she will curl her fingers into your skin, dragging down to leave her mark. Just as you did with her, she'll put her palm over the mark until it is cool. Once both mates are marked, the mating is complete and is forever binding. The two souls will irrevocably be joined."

Dominic jerked in his seat when the loud shrill of the emergency phone filled the room and ended the conversation. Without missing a beat at all, Dominic followed Conner out the door; he was rather grateful for the break. He needed time to process what they'd discussed and to try his hand at Dream Bonding.

Sunshine, Victoria, Australia

Cancer.

The Big C.

Adele allowed the words to echo around her mind as she struggled to breathe through her grief. The disease was so far advanced there was no hope of finding a suitable treatment. Guilt had her stomach roiling and bile rising up her throat. Had she been so preoccupied with study she hadn't noticed how sick her mother had become? She'd noticed her mother looking tired lately, but when she asked her about it, her mother told her how working two jobs was tiring and she just needed some more sleep. It was nothing for Adele to worry about. According to her mother, Adele had enough to worry about with her University exams. Had her mother known? Had she hidden it from her? Her only daughter?

Now, Adele was the one who was bone-tired. Her stiff and aching muscles reminded her she'd been sitting by her mother's bed for the past four days. She was praying and waiting for her mother to wake up or give her some kind of sign that she was still with her.

She hated the way the nurses and doctors looked at her with big sad eyes. Adele wasn't ready to accept her new reality. It was too much for her to bear on her own. At least her mother wasn't in any pain. The doctor had assured Adele of it and it had eased the vice on her heart a fraction. She'd seen the staff making sure her mother had enough morphine in her system to ease her pain. During her Nursing Degree, she'd learned about Palliative Care and she'd thought it seemed like such a nice and easy concept. Now, those two words tore her heart and soul to shreds quicker than she'd ever thought possible.

With silent tears tracking down her face and falling on the crisp white hospital sheet, she said a quiet plea, using her mother's native French in an attempt to rouse her.

"S'il te plaît, réveille-toi maman, ne me quitte pas sans dire au revoir."

Please wake up, Mama...don't leave me without saying goodbye.

Weariness tugged at her mind until she gave in and laid her head down next to her mother's hand, which she held in her own. Tears stained her cheeks until her exhaustion pulled her into sleep.

Adele woke to the sounds of the bush. Birds called and wind rustled leaves. Opening her eyes, she found herself surrounded by some of the tallest, straightest gum trees she'd ever seen. She was lying on her back on soft native grass in a small clearing and directly above her was a gorgeous cloudless blue sky. Tension eased out of her body as she allowed herself to relax; this place was beautiful and so peaceful. The sun felt so warm on her face and bare arms. She closed her eyes to enjoy the warmth as she took a deep breath of clean country air. With each exhale, she calmed more while all the real world stresses began to fall away. She had no idea how her mind had managed to create this place, one she had never seen before, but she was grateful for it.

She flicked her eyes wide open as she sensed someone watching her. She held her breath as she slowly sat up, turning her head to each side to look around the clearing and over the lake in front of her.

Her movements froze when she heard a noise that sounded distinctly like purring. Very loud, very close purring. She swung her head toward the sound and came face to face with a cat. No, not a cat, or at least not a house cat. This was a wild animal and he was huge and extremely beautiful. His large head was level with hers as he sat watching her with an intense stare. His fur looked so soft. His chest was pure white while the rest of his coat was tinged with brown and had black-grey spots.

Adele's gaze got caught in his once more. Ice blue orbs glowing with intelligence, protection, and compassion. A wave of calm flowed through her as she sat mesmerized, which was plain crazy. After all, she was sitting in front of a snow leopard, for crying out loud! Even for her imagination, this was astounding.

She wondered if she should be afraid, run as fast and as far away as she could, but this was only a dream, so it was safe. That, and for some strange reason she felt compelled to remain close to this beautiful animal.

Purring, the leopard slowly stood and padded over to her. Her heart racing in anticipation, she remained frozen to the spot as she waited to see what he was going to do next. He nuzzled his head up her leg as he lay down by her side. He pushed his back into her as he continued to nuzzle against her thigh.

It felt so good and within moments her heart rate settled back to normal and the tension flowed from her muscles once again. Speechless, she gazed down his long body, and he was definitely a boy leopard. She reached out and rubbed his fluffy ear and stroked his soft cheek, pushing back his thick white whiskers. His purring got louder and he closed his eyes as he nuzzled against her palm.

Totally surreal.

She couldn't put her finger on how she knew, but she was certain he was her guardian. There was definitely a connection between her and the animal, like her soul recognized him. It was a bizarre feeling knowing this snow leopard was somehow hers.

Her chaton, *her kitten.*

After stroking and petting him for several minutes, she was so relaxed that her mind began to wonder. Reality crept in on her thoughts and she couldn't help the sob that escaped her throat. Her mother, her whole world, was dying. She let go of the leopard, brought her knees up, and buried her face in her hands. And let out gut-wrenching sobs that shook her whole being.

The sudden coolness against her leg let her know the leopard had moved away from her. She guessed he didn't appreciate a crying woman. She didn't care. She needed to let out all the pain that was tearing her apart inside and eating her alive.

While lost in her pain and tears she gasped when warmth surrounded her. He hadn't left her at all. He'd just moved so he could curl himself around her so she was cradled between his front and back legs. Butterflies took flight in her tummy as she realized the leopard was trying to cuddle her. Hiccupping as her sobs receded, she raised her head out of her hands and wiped her eyes with her fingers. A nudge at her arm followed by a whimper had her looking into his face through her watery gaze. Her throat tightened at the concern and kindness that shone from his ice-blue irises. Was he for real? This didn't feel like a normal dream. Could the animal understand her, could he actually care for her?

"Are you really here? Just for me, my chaton?*" she whispered.*

He responded by nuzzling her shoulder and giving her neck a little lick that tickled. A snort broke free from her unbidden and had the animal purring.

"You like me giggling, do you?"

A small smile tugged at her lips when he nuzzled his head under her arm, until he was resting on her lap.

"You're just a little pushy, my chaton,*" she said, lowering her legs to make room for him. She stroked the silky soft fur on the top of his head, between his ears.*

She could really use a hug. She moved herself down so she could lie with her head on his shoulder. He moved with her so she lay on her side against his hind leg with her head positioned just behind his shoulder. She stroked the thick fur down his front leg and paw, tracing his spots then the pads of his foot.

She watched as her tears landed on his soft fur. Words tumbled from her lips before she realized it.

"She's dying. My precious mother is leaving me," she whispered.

"She's all I have. I'm going to be so alone once she's gone."

As she poured her heart out, her chaton *gently nuzzled her cheek and shoulder. Eventually her tears ran out and with the sun warming her from above, and her* chaton *warming her from below, exhaustion made her heavy eyelids close. With his purring filling her mind, she felt safe and protected. Maybe she wasn't totally alone in the world after all.*

Dominic watched Conner hoe into his breakfast of bacon and eggs as he came into the kitchen. Their mother put a plate identical to his brother's down on the table for him as she gave him a quick kiss on the cheek.

"You're looking better this morning, my darling son, did your father's advice help?"

Dominic chuckled softly as he noticed Conner had stopped with his fork halfway to his mouth. He watched Dominic with avid interest. Obviously, he was desperate to know if the Dream Bonding their father had told them about had worked. No doubt he was trying to soak in all the information he could, hopeful that he would soon dream of his own mate. At nineteen, Conner still had at least a couple of years to go. Male shifters were always older than their mates.

"Breakfast smells great, thanks, Mum." He gave his mum a kiss on the cheek before he sat down. "Yeah, Dad's advice was definitely helpful. I managed to get the Dream Bonding to work last night. Took me a bit to get it started but, damn, was it well worth the effort," he answered with a broad grin.

This morning he'd woken feeling lighter and more relaxed than he had been in weeks. A little shiver ran up his spine as he recalled how good it had felt to have her hands in his fur. The knowledge that she wasn't in any imminent danger was a huge relief, although he hated that she was emotionally hurting.

"I'm glad to hear it, Dominic. Next time you won't wait so long before going to your father for help, will you?" She didn't wait for him to answer before she continued, "I've got to get moving, so I'll leave you boys to it. Shopping doesn't do itself and with the way you boys and your father eat, you have no idea how much I wish it did. I'll catch you both later."

She gave both her sons a kiss on the top of their heads.

"Now don't you boys forget to put your dishes in the dishwasher before you leave."

"Shall do, Mum."

Dominic smirked when he and Conner spoke at the same time. Then silence filled the room and as Dominic continued to eat, he barely held back from laughing. Clearly, Conner wanted to ask him about what happened but was trying to act cool. He knew his little brother wouldn't be able to resist for long.

Sure enough, after a few minutes Conner cracked and started the anticipated questioning.

"So, what happened, Dom? Is she all right? Do you know where to find her now?"

Dominic remained silent for a minute while he finished off his mouthful, enjoying the show of his brother squirming in anticipation. But he could only torture his little brother for so long. Besides, he really wanted to share what he had learned with his brother, who was also his best friend.

"I was right, Conner. My sweet mate is hurting something fierce. She told me her mother was dying and that it's always been just the two of them. She's feeling like she's going to be alone when her mother dies."

Conner frowned at him.

"She told you all that? In one dream—to a man she's never seen before? Dream Bonding's that strong, huh?"

Dominic barked out a laugh. "Hell no, even in dreams women don't tell strange men anything. I did try to join her dream as a man while she was dreaming of a public place, but she just moved past me, refusing to even look at me even when I called out. It was obvious she has little interest in men in general. I'm thinking maybe she's been hurt by a man at some point; her dad maybe? If it's just her and her mum, her dad's obviously not in the picture." He didn't want to even contemplate it being an ex-boyfriend. "So anyway, when that didn't work I tried pulling her into my dream. That worked perfectly. I took her to the little field up near the lake and met her in my leopard form."

"Oh man, you trying to make the woman run?" Conner's voice was laced with humor as he slapped his thighs.

"It wasn't like I had much choice, Conner. It's either man or leopard, and she didn't want the man. But she didn't run. After a little bit she cuddled up to me, spilled her story, had a good cry, then closed her eyes and relaxed with her head over my heart and her hand buried in my fur. Man, was I one happy cat. I got to see all of her, from head to toe and, Conner, she looks just like an angel. She had her dark wavy hair spread across my fur, and her ivory skin looked so soft. Even with her warm chocolate-colored eyes closed, I could still feel their warmth." Dominic's eyes glazed over as he sighed.

"Don't know that I ever want to be mated if I have to look like you do right now, bro. You look like a bloody lovesick kitten."

Conner rolled his eyes with a dramatic shudder Dominic knew he was putting on. Dominic's lips quirked into a lopsided grin as he remembered his mate's nickname for him.

"You know, that's what she called me. Her *chaton*. I looked it up this morning. It's French for kitten."

That had Conner instantly roaring with laughter, and Dominic couldn't help but join his brother. He just hoped like hell that he didn't have to wait too long before he would meet his mate in real life.

Chapter One

The gravel crunched under the soles of Adele's shoes as she walked through the cemetery. She slowed down as she approached the row where her mother's grave lay. She rubbed her fist over her aching heart; she still struggled to accept her mother was really gone. Her vision blurred with tears as she left the path to walk over the grass toward her mother. Frustrated, she swiped at the tears with her free hand. Surely after four years she shouldn't continue to fall apart at the mere thought of her mother?

Adele didn't bother looking where she was going. She'd been to her mother's grave so many times she was quite sure she could now find it while blindfolded in the dark. Her stomach twisted in knots of grief, she reached her mother's grave. Doing her best to push aside her roiling emotions, she set about cleaning the tombstone off and neatening it up. Then she carefully placed her six deep purple roses, her mother's favorite, in the special vase built into the top.

Once that was taken care of, she crumpled to her knees on the grass and let the tight hold on her emotions go. As her tears began to flow, she buried her face in her hands. Four years later, the wound to her heart and soul still felt so fresh, like it had remained open and continued to bleed.

"Ma chère maman, tu me manques beaucoup."

My precious mother, I miss you so much.

As she'd always done, she spoke to her mother in French, taking comfort in using her mother's native language.

After several minutes, she managed to rein in her emotions. She pulled out a tissue, dried her eyes, blew her nose, and took a few deep breaths. She had things to tell her mother but she couldn't afford to sit here all day in the sun, she had studying to do. Opening her eyes, she looked up at the tombstone, reading the words she had so carefully chosen four years ago:

'In Ever Loving Memory Of
Fleur Petit
26-5-1972 - 20-11-2007
Loving Mother of Adele
As a mother you cared for me,
the Lord will now care for you.'

In a quiet whisper, Adele told her mother everything that had happened since she visited a fortnight ago.

"I'm nearly finished, *Maman*. My last exam is on Thursday, then I'm all done with Uni. You'd be so proud. I got my honors completed too. Your *petit fille* will soon be a qualified nurse and paramedic. If only I could find a job." She sighed. "I think I'm going to have to leave Sunshine."

The thought of leaving left her heart aching, but staying here surrounded by memories and reminders of her mother wouldn't be any easier. It had been unbearable at times over the last four years. Now, with University nearly over, she could feel the beginnings of depression claw at her. She needed to get away, get a fresh start or she would remain stuck in her mother's shadow, forever grieving and never moving on with her own life.

"I've found a few openings coming up in Tasmania. I've applied in Devonport, Strahan, Rosebery, and Hobart. I'm sure I'll be able to land one of them. I think I'll like Tasmania. It doesn't get as hot in the summer, for one thing. You know how well me and summer heat get along. Most of the jobs aren't going to start until the new year so I've got time to finish up Uni before moving over. I figure, new year, new start—what better time to go."

Tears pricked her eyes again when she realized she wouldn't be able to come for her fortnightly visits with her *Maman* anymore. But maybe that was part of the problem; she needed some distance to allow her heart to heal.

"I'm going to miss being able to visit you. I thought maybe if I take a photo, I can still sit and talk with you. I spoke with Chrissy and she's going to come visit on your birthday each year and tidy up for us."

Brushing away tears, Adele glanced down at her watch and gasped at how much time had passed. Time always seemed to fly when she was with her mother.

"Okay, *Maman*, I've got to get moving. I need to study for my exams. I don't think I'll be able to visit as usual, but I promise I'll come and see you again before I leave."

Adele stood and with a wince, stretched out her muscles that were cramping from sitting down for so long. With a lump in her throat, she laid a soft kiss to the top of the tombstone before heading back toward her car.

As Adele reached for her car door a tingle of awareness run up her spine. With a frown, she turned back toward the cemetery and froze as she tried to wrap her mind around what she saw. Was that a leopard under the tree near her mother's grave? She rubbed her eyes, before she looked again. Nothing out of the ordinary was there. She shook her head and climbed into her car. She was getting way too caught up in her dreams if she was imagining leopards in real life.

Cradle Mountains National Park, Tasmania, Australia

Dominic's muscles relaxed as he took a deep breath of cool fresh mountain air. He didn't get to do this nearly as often as he would like to. In his teenage years, after he first shifted at fifteen, he would go for runs through the mountains regularly, but as he'd gotten older adult responsibilities had filled his time.

Nothing felt better than having the wind over his face as he ran through the scrub. Or the way water splashed up on his paws and stomach cooling him off as he loped through the creeks. He arrived at the top of a high cliff and a shiver ran down his spine as he took in the natural beauty of the

Cradle Mountains. Awareness seeped into him a moment before he heard a quiet growl to his right. He grunted but stayed still when Conner head-butted his shoulder.

What's up, Dominic? I can feel your anguish.

Some days Dominic could do without the connections shifters had when in leopard form. Since members of the same Leap could project their thoughts to each other, they could also get a sense of each other's emotions. Today of all days, he didn't want everyone knowing how he was feeling.

My mate was really hurting yesterday. It was the fourth anniversary of her mother's death. Just like Dad told us, I felt her pain like it's my own. I just wish she'd come to me or given me some hint to where she is so I could go get her. It's driving me insane being able to feel her pain but not being able to do anything to comfort her.

Wow. It's been four years already? Surely you'll meet her soon, bro. How long until you go search for her?

Soon, I can't wait much longer. After the fire season is finished I'll head over to the mainland and start searching. He didn't want to leave Rosebery, this was his home and where his Leap was. It was tearing up his insides not being able to hold his mate. *Come on, let's go for another run before it gets late and we have to head home.*

Conner nipped the back of Dominic's hind leg before leaping off through the bush. With a playful growl, Dominic took off after his brother— Conner was so going to pay for that cheap shot.

Dominic let Conner lead the way for a few minutes before he sped up and leapt onto his back, grabbing his neck with his teeth, gently of course; he would never intentionally hurt his brother, and rolled to the ground with him. Dominic loved mucking around with his brother. They both gave in to their inner kittens and rolled around play fighting, growling, and purring. It was a good ten minutes before Dominic decided to end things and pinned Conner down.

C'mon, Conner, sun's setting. We better get moving. Thanks for the game, bro.

After lightly tapping his head against his brother's, Dominic leapt to the side, releasing Conner before they leisurely prowled back to the carpark. As they got near, they stopped to listen for any humans close by. Dominic couldn't sense anyone close but it always paid to play it safe. They shifted back to human form before emerging from the trees. Better if they got busted as naked humans than as snow leopards if there was anybody around.

Dominic led Conner through the tree line and was relieved to discover they were indeed alone. A shiver ran through him as the wind whipped around him.

"Damn, it's cold with no fur," Dominic complained.

"Tell me about it."

Dressing quickly, he wasted no time jumping into his car so he could crank on the heat before he drove his brother home. Dominic felt a hell of a lot better after their day out and a quick glance at Conner confirmed that he too was looking more relaxed and at ease than he had looked before they went out.

Cole Jones was hot and frustrated. Neither of those things helped his mood, in fact, they sent it straight down the drain. Just like every other damn day down at the Strahan Docks, he'd loaded and unloaded containers all day. What made today particularly crappy was that summer had kicked in early, throwing a stinking hot day at him in November. Out on the docks under the sun, it felt like the inside of an oven and that always put everyone on edge. Which meant, not only was he in a hellish mood, but so was everyone else, and he didn't have the patience for any of it.

Maybe he should have finished school, gotten himself a fancy desk job in a climate controlled office. Damn, what he wouldn't give for an air conditioner right about now. His belly tightened as his mind wondered to other things.

Finding a way to cool down wasn't the only thing that would improve his terrible day. He cracked his knuckles. A good solid workout followed up with a hard fuck would definitely improve his mood. Thoughts of how he'd spend his evening kept his mind happily occupied for the rest of the day. He didn't bother saying goodbye to anyone, that would take time and he just wanted to get home. Jumping in his ute, he wasted no time in cranking over the engine and roaring out of the carpark. His blood buzzed with anticipation of what he would do when he arrived home.

When he turned into his driveway, his left hand started to tremble. He took a deep breath and tamped down his excitement. He wanted his fun to last tonight, so he needed to settle down before he got started.

After parking his ute in the garage and making sure it was locked up, he walked up the path and pushed through the front door. His house wasn't huge. The main living area was open plan, with the kitchen at one end and lounge at the other. Three bedrooms and a bathroom came off the main room, and of course, the downstairs basement that had a small hallway and two rooms. The open plan suited his needs perfectly. It meant that by collaring the slave and chaining her on a fifty-foot chain she could do all he needed her to, but couldn't get out the front door and escape.

As he entered, he saw the brat silently slide into her room. Good. He didn't want to deal with her tonight. He wanted the slave. He rolled his shoulder anticipating his workout, hearing her screams. He continued his way through the house until he found what he was looking for. She was in the kitchen, trembling by the oven. He stalked over to her until he stood over her much smaller body, relishing her fear soaked wide eyed expression she looked up at him with. She was right to fear him in this moment. He was in one hell of a ferocious mood tonight. He cracked his knuckles, loving how she shuddered in response.

"I - I - I've made dinner for you, just like you wanted," she stammered.

Perfect. He grinned as a thrill ran through him. She was trying to placate him into not taking her downstairs; after all these years she really should know better. His moods were only placated by working her body over and fucking her.

"Turn everything off. You've got somewhere else to be."

Even he could hear excitement in his voice. Which made sense. He couldn't wait to get her downstairs. Arms crossed over his chest, he watched her hands tremble as she struggled to turn off the oven before taking the pot over to the sink. As soon as her hands left the metal, he pounced on her. Wrapping his fingers in her soft hair, he used it to drag her to the door that led to his basement wonderland. He only paused long enough to unlock the chain from her collar and carefully hang it on the hook by the door. His OCD could be such a bitch but he knew if he left it in a mess, he wouldn't be able to fully focus on what he was about to do. With each step he took down, his blood burned hotter as he thought over exactly what he was going to do.

Detective Alex Ross stared down at the reports he'd spread out over his desk. His heart clenched. So many lives cut short. Each of the eight profiles had a confirmed identity so they had photos of how each woman had looked alive. Grainy driver's license photos and blurry year book snaps glared up at him, as if the victims knew their killer hadn't been brought to justice yet. Then there were the police photos. The ones of beaten and battered bodies dragged from the river or ocean.

The first time he'd read these damned reports he'd thrown up. Each time he had to work on them bile rose up his throat. Alex was raised to respect all life, but in particular to protect women and children. He entered the police force so he could uphold those beliefs and every time he had to deal with domestic violence or a particularly horrific murder, his soul screamed at the injustice. Especially when they couldn't catch the damn perpetrator and the bastard kept doing it.

This particular bastard had to live around Strahan somewhere. He'd been raping and killing women for ten years, at least. Alex had always believed these cases were linked, and so did most of the cops who'd had anything to do with any of these murders, but they had no proof. Each of the bodies had been found in either the river or the ocean near Strahan so any evidence was compromised with water damage. Unfortunately for the perpetrator, technology was getting better at pulling DNA from the smallest of samples. A thrill ran through him as he looked over the newest report. The DNA profile of the killer. They nearly had him. All they needed to do now was find the match. Naturally, it wasn't in the system. Alex rolled his eyes, even though he was alone. That would make things way too simple.

But they did have a profile on him. One that stated the man most likely worked near the water. That he was middle-aged and would have control issues. Alex had already compiled the list of businesses that were on or near the coast or river. The biggest was the Strahan Docks, which thankfully ran random drug tests on their employees. Alex was hopeful he could get a judge to agree to give him an order for the Docks to hand over their next round of tests for DNA analysis. Hopefully he'd find a match and put this killer behind bars where he belonged.

As he moved to his computer to fill out the relevant paperwork, the photo on his desk caught his attention. He'd taken it on their last family holiday, his wife and two beautiful teenage daughters were smiling at him, looking happy and carefree. Something these eight women would never be again. His resolve to find this bastard before he could strike again strengthened. He had to catch him before he took any more lives.

Blood and pain always makes sex better. Hell, they made life better, Cole mused to himself. He unhooked the slave's cuffs and watched with satisfaction as she slumped down on the floor. Damn, he felt good. So much better than earlier.

He pulled his pants back on as the slave attempted to stand. His lip curled into a sneer; she was so weak and unworthy of a master like him. He needed a stronger slave, one that could handle the workouts and rough fucking. Although, this one had lasted longer than most. She was still lacking in so many ways. Growling, he grabbed her arm in a tight grip and roughly hauled her back up the stairs. She tripped twice but he refused to slow or allow her any time to get her feet back under her. He simply kept a tight grip on her and dragged her up. Once out, he closed the door and carefully reattached the chain to her collar before shoving her aside.

"You've got fifteen minutes to get cleaned up and serve me dinner, or back down you go."

He needed a drink, but couldn't stand the thought of the slave getting blood all over the bottle. The only mess he allowed was downstairs. Keeping that room bloodstained helped him torture his slaves so much better. Everywhere else was a different story. He required his home to be meticulously clean and he certainly wouldn't stand for drinking from a dirty bottle.

He tore open the fridge and snatched a cold bottle of beer before he headed to the lounge for some chill out time in front of the TV. A haze of red clouded his vision for a moment when he noticed the TV was already on—bloody cartoons, damn little brat. He wondered where she was, before shaking his head. Who the fuck cared. He did appreciate that the brat knew to hide, knew to stay silent. He'd always hated kids, detested having to put up with their noise and mess. But this one's sad, lonely, desperate mother, who had no family or friends had been too easy to entrap to resist. No one had noticed her not hanging around town anymore. No one had filed a missing person's report on either of them. He took a long swallow of beer, letting the cool liquid calm him further. He supposed the slave's little brat wasn't too bad. She was certainly pretty, with her black curls and big round grey eyes. Such a pity she was too young for his tastes. He was sure she'd make a better slave than her useless mother. Those big grey eyes wide in pain would be a thing to see. That got his mind ticking over, maybe when the brat was older and her mother had passed being useful, he could get rid of her and train the brat to be his slave, properly. His very own virginal slave...he chuckled, yeah that sounded fucking ace.

Kelly silently closed her door as she heard his evil chuckle, the one that always made the hairs on her neck stand up and her body shudder. She'd heard his heavy footsteps on the stairs as he'd dragged her mother back up minutes ago. As always, she'd been listening for it and silently fled to her bedroom away from the lounge where she had the TV on trying to drown out the sounds of her mother screaming. A violent shudder ran through her body. She heard those screams in her nightmares each night.

Once safely in her room, panic had her sweating. She'd forgotten to turn the TV off. Her heart had just about beat out of her chest as she'd waited on his reaction. Thankfully, she'd been lucky this time. All he'd done was curse before changing the channel.

A ragged sigh escaped her lips. He hadn't come looking for her like she feared he would one of these days. He'd never touched her. He rarely even spoke to her. But she could see the violence in his eyes. Saw the condition her mother was constantly in from his *attention*.

Kelly slid down the wall, sitting with her knees up and her head back against the plaster. Instinctively trying to make herself smaller. The shirt she wore pulled tight against her throat and she tugged at it. She'd outgrown her stolen clothing again. She needed to sneak out and get herself something bigger. No doubt, her mother would need new clothing after tonight too.

A couple of years ago, after going out while he was at work, she'd discovered a clothing bin a few streets away. Since then, she would sneak out every six months or so and get herself bigger clothes. She also brought some back for her mother each time. He was always ripping her mother's clothes, wrecking them. He didn't allow them to leave the house, didn't provide anything more than food. Fortunately, he didn't pay any attention to what they did or didn't wear either, so he didn't notice when she'd been out to get more.

She closed her eyes and floated back in time. Five years ago, she and her mother were on the run from her father when they'd met Him. Her mother, tired of running, of being alone, was desperate. When he offered them the use of his 'unused small house on the outskirts of town' her mother told her this was a sign that all their problems were over. Yeah, right. Problems over. She grunted. The house was meant to be empty, just the two of them living there, starting afresh. When they arrived to move in he'd been there waiting for them. Had a collar and chain on her mother in a flash and since then they had both been enslaved. Kelly could leave, she wasn't physically chained, but she could never abandon her mother. Her mother would always need Kelly to help her. Just like after her father had finished with her, Kelly would clean up her mother when He was done. Help her recover and heal up. She needed to go to the bathroom to see how she could help.

She had learned how to move without a sound soon after she learned to walk and the skill continued to serve her well. She silently made her way to the bathroom. She didn't want him to notice her. She was getting older now, starting to develop lady parts. If she wasn't careful, he would notice and then she would end up being dragged down those horrid stairs to where very bad things happened. And she was quite certain she wanted to avoid that outcome at all costs.

Find all the buy links for Guardian's Heart at:

http://khloewren.com/GuardiansHeart

CPSIA information can be obtained
at www.ICGtesting.com
Printed in the USA
FFHW010048030519
52218948-57608FF